DOUBLE-YUCK MAGIC

KATHLEEN DUEY lives in the middle of an avocado and persimmon grove with her husband and two sons. When the moon is full and the coyotes are howling, she sits at her computer and believes in magic.

DOUBLE-YUCK MAGIC

KATHLEEN DUEY

AN AVON CAMELOT BOOK

To my parents, Bill Peery and Mary E. Peery,
with love

DOUBLE-YUCK MAGIC is an original publication of Avon Books. This work has never before appeared in book form.

AVON BOOKS
A division of
The Hearst Corporation
1350 Avenue of the Americas
New York, New York 10019

Copyright © 1991 by Kathleen Duey
Published by arrangement with the author
Library of Congress Catalog Card Number: 91-92062
ISBN: 0-380-76116-5
RL: 4.5

First Avon Camelot Printing: November 1991

CAMELOT TRADEMARK REG. U.S. PAT. OFF. AND IN OTHER COUNTRIES, MARCA REGISTRADA, HECHO EN U.S.A.

Printed in the U.S.A.

OPM 10 9 8 7 6 5 4 3 2 1

CHAPTER ONE

When we moved into our new apartment, I wasn't thinking about magic. I was thinking about trying to stay out of trouble. I try to follow the rules. I really do. But it almost never works out for me. It sure didn't this time. I guess it all started because I get a little lonely.

I'm an only child. Sometimes other kids say that I'm lucky not to have brothers and sisters, but there are disadvantages, too. Think about it. Imagine being the only kid in the house. Who gets blamed for everything? You, that's who. Who's the one your parents worry about all the time? You, of course. If your parents read some new book about how to raise kids better, who gets to be the star of the experiment? You. You're the only one they've got.

And if they have some awful old family name they want to pass on, like Mathilda, guess who gets it? My name is Mathilda Olivia Jameson. My parents wanted to name someone after dear old great-grandmother Mathilda Olivia Jameson. I was the only kid available for the honor. Lucky me.

I always tell people that my name is Matt. If they

think that's a strange name for a girl, that's their problem. *Anything* is better than being called Mathilda.

Since I was really little, I've wanted a dog. I like dogs a lot, but we've always lived in apartment buildings—and there's always a rule against having pets. Most landlords don't even want kids in their buildings. Old Mr. Norris, our landlord, doesn't like kids. And he *hates* dogs. I will never forget the first time I met him. It was on the first day we moved here, before all the magic stuff got started.

My dad was at a meeting. My mom and I had been carrying boxes for hours. On the last trip up in the elevator, I was so stacked with boxes that I couldn't see where I was going. I was tired, too. I leaned against the back wall of the elevator until it stopped. My mother nudged me forward and I stumbled into the hall. She tried to steady me, but her load was even bigger than mine. We bumped back and forth, bouncing off the walls and each other for a minute before we finally got headed in the right direction.

Our new apartment still smelled like fresh paint. Mom dumped her stuff on the couch. I set my boxes in a teetering stack on top of hers. There were cartons and boxes everywhere.

Mom sat down on a pile of sheets and pillows and sighed. Then she brightened up and smiled. "You know, Matt, I really like this place."

I nodded. It wasn't bad. The neighborhood was pretty and there was a big park a couple of blocks away. The apartment had big windows, and the ceilings had those fancy, old-fashioned designs in the plaster. The whole building was old. It was red brick, kind of stained looking. My mother had liked that when we first came to look at it. She said it had character.

2

Mom was tapping her fingers on a cardboard box, frowning the way she does when she's about to say something serious. "I want you to think about something, Matt," she said slowly. "This place was very hard to find, and it's nearly perfect. It would be almost impossible to find another apartment this perfect."

What she meant was that I had better stay out of trouble. My parents never come right out and say it, but when we have to move, it's almost always my fault. They hate moving, because we have a lot of stuff to move. And I mean *a lot.*

My mother works in a biogenetic laboratory. She's a scientist and everybody says she's really smart. I guess she is. But when it comes to collecting junk, she is unbelievable. She goes to auctions and antique sales, garage sales and second hand stores. She buys all kinds of interesting stuff. She also buys a lot of junk that isn't interesting at all. That would be okay if she would ever admit it and throw some things away, but she almost never does.

We have enough old books to fill a bookstore, and our closets are so crammed that just opening the doors can be dangerous. You never know what might fall off the top shelf and bash you on the head. It could be a computer monitor or a butter churn. But *something* will fall, and you'd better jump.

My parents never knew it, but my whole space project last year was built straight out of our closets. Except the fuel, of course, but that was easy enough to get. I'm still proud of the fuel system I designed—but I goofed somewhere in the ignition wiring. After they repaired the ceiling in our old apartment, you couldn't tell that a rocket had been launched there by mistake. I corrected the ignition problem, but the landlord refused to believe that it would never happen again. We were asked to move. So we were moving. All the boxes were up here now. It was time to unpack.

I glanced at my mother. She was sitting back, her eyes closed. I started to lean back, too. "Okay," she said without opening her eyes. "Time to get going. I'll start in my room, you start in yours."

I stood up and headed down the hall, then I heard the doorbell ring. Mom answered it and I saw a grumpy-looking man with gray hair. He was carrying a toolbox. Mom motioned at me. She was smiling, but her lips looked stiff. "Mr. Norris, this is Mathilda," she said.

"Matt," I said automatically. I held out my hand. Ever since I turned twelve, I've been shaking hands with people. It helps them remember that I'm not a kid anymore.

"Mr. Norris is our landlord," my mother said, still smiling. I know that smile. She smiles like that when she wants me to be polite, say as little as possible, and not cause trouble of any kind. It's a very nervous smile. I try not to cause trouble. But sometimes it's hard—like when adults are rude when I'm trying to be polite. Mr. Norris didn't shake hands with me. He just looked at my hand and frowned.

I sighed. I didn't like Mr. Norris and I could tell he didn't like me—and we had just met. There didn't seem to be anything to lose so I asked my standard question. I always ask, just in case.

"Can I have a dog here?"

Mr. Norris set down his toolbox with a little clank. He stared down at me. He had started out looking grumpy. Now he looked almost mean. He had bushy

4

eyebrows and he looked like a bulldog, as if he couldn't smile even if he wanted to.

"I have a rule against animals in the building," he said. His voice was rough and raspy. "Especially dogs. They're destructive and noisy, and they're filthy."

He sounded like he was reciting the Constitution or something. I opened my mouth to answer him, but my mother gave me a *look*. I know that look. It means, "Matt, please. Close your mouth." So I closed my mouth. But I did it for my mom, not for Mr. Norris. I didn't like him at all.

"Let me know if you need anything, Mrs. Jameson," he said to my mother.

"I've told Matt that if she ever forgets her key that she can ask you to let her in with your passkey," my mother said.

Mr. Norris was frowning. "I will, but I hope it won't happen too often." Then he looked at me again. "I think we'll get along." It sounded like a threat, the way he said it. He nodded at my mother and left.

"Try to stay on his good side," my mother said gently.

"I don't think he *has* one," I muttered, but she went right on talking.

"Just try to stay out of trouble, Matt. We need this place. It's so close to your new school and . . ."

I nodded fast to make her stop. I didn't want to talk about the new school. I didn't even want to *think* about it.

"I'm sorry about the dog," Mom was saying. "But you knew what he would say, and, Matt, in a way he's right. An apartment really isn't a good place for a dog." She ruffled my hair with her hand.

I stepped away from her. I know she does it to let

5

me know she loves me, but hair ruffling is a little silly for someone my age. "Boxes," I said, in a quivery, funny voice to make her laugh. "There are dozens of evil boxes waiting for us."

She laughed. "Okay, okay. Back to work."

I went down the hall and flopped onto my unmade bed, trying not to think about the new school. At least I liked my room. It was a soft blue color and it smelled clean, like new paint. One whole wall was built-in bookshelves. There was a big window that faced the street. I stood up and looked out. Over the rooftops I could see the green of the trees in the park. Right across the street from the park was Tillison School for troublemakers.

They didn't call it that, of course, but I knew that's what it was. I had never been to a private school in my entire life and I wasn't looking forward to it now. Besides, I hate being the new kid at school. Kids usually tease me about my name . . . or about being smart or because I get into trouble a lot. I flopped back onto my bed. Mom and Dad said that I was getting bored in public school, and that Tillison would challenge me. Tillison didn't really have grades—you worked at whatever level the teachers thought you could handle.

I was kind of bored a lot of the time, but it didn't matter what my parents said about challenges and all the rest. I knew why they were sending me to Tillison. I had heard them talking. They wanted teachers who could *direct* my energy and intelligence into *positive experiences*—and keep me out of trouble.

Yuck and double yuck. That's another disadvantage of being an only child. They really want you to be a big deal, so they can be proud of you. You're their only chance, see? Positive experiences and good nutrition and real achievement and all the rest. I tried to talk them out of it at first, but they made it very clear that I was going to go to Tillison School this year and that was that. Period.

But maybe I wouldn't get teased so much at Tillison School. After all, everybody there had probably caused trouble somewhere. If they had been doing fine in public school, their parents would have left them there, right? Who wants to pay a bunch of money so that a kid can take a few advanced courses a few years earlier? I was staring at the boxes stacked on the floor. I made myself get up and start unpacking clothes . . . but I couldn't stop thinking. I never managed to stay out of trouble for very long—no matter how hard I tried.

Once, when I was about five, I decided to collect butterflies and moths. They were pretty unusual pets, I guess, but they were the only pets I could think of that weren't against the rules. I collected a lot of them. I liked the soft, whirring sound that they made flying around. Then one day my mother came into my room. She was saying something, I could see her lips moving, but I couldn't hear her too well. I told her to speak up.

"Oh pena win dough," she shouted through the whirring.

"What, Mommy?" I shouted back. I was pretty little.

She just shook her head and waved her hands back and forth and tried to open the window, but I had taped it shut so my butterflies and moths couldn't escape. All of a sudden I could see my mother better, and I knew what was happening. So did she, a second later. She had left the door wide open. She ran to close it but it was too late.

It might have worked out better if I hadn't opened the front door into the hallway. But I was only five, after all, and Mom seemed so upset about all the moths and butterflies in the living room that I just wanted to get them out. Once they were in the hallway, the problems got worse. The landlord said there was a lot of damage caused by caterpillars in the lights and smoke alarms and thermostats. I guess most of my moths laid eggs. Later, there were cocoons plugging up the heating system. The landlord said that he should make us pay for fixing everything. He also said that we would have to move. Back then, I thought it was pretty funny . . . having to move like that. Now I know it wasn't. I got up and forced myself to concentrate on hanging up clothes.

"Are you working?" my mother called down the hallway. I heard thumps and a rubbing sound and she appeared in the doorway dragging an enormous box behind her.

"My bookshelves are full, and you have room," she said as she straightened up. I looked at the wall. The built-in bookshelves ran from the ceiling to the floor of my room. I tried to smile. I knew that box. It was full of books. Her garage sale treasures. In our last apartment it had been in the hall. There were two others just like it. I knew what she was thinking.

"How about the closet in your room?" I asked hopefully.

She shook her head. "No. Come on, Matt. I'm too tired to argue. Please. I want to get them out of the boxes." She pointed at the box. "I packed your books in here too."

8

I swallowed and nodded, giving up. I would have room on my bookshelves, and her closets would be full of other things. Very full. As always. She smiled and left, then came back, dragging the other two boxes. I stared at them for a minute before I looked in the first box and groaned. My books were on top, all right, but there had to be fifty of hers underneath. At least. "Thanks Matt," my mother said as she went out the door.

I set my astronomy books into the top shelves. Then there were the ones on biology and computer programming and chemistry. And all the archaeology books from my dad. I had some books from when I was younger too. Books about dogs. Books about how to take care of them and stories about dogs, too. I hugged one old storybook before I put it up on the shelf. My parents gave it to me when I was about five. It has a picture of a dog on the cover. He has curly cream-colored fur and bright brown eyes. When I was little I named him Jaspar, and if I ever get to have a dog that's what I want him to look like. Every time we move, I pack that old storybook. I suddenly felt like crying. So I reached down and got out an armload of my mother's books and started looking through the titles.

They were impossible to sort, because Mom buys anything and everything. There was one book on Volkswagen repair. We have never owned a Volkswagen. There was one about how to make cheese from raw goat's milk. I don't know if my mother has ever seen a goat. Maybe at the zoo. There was book about knitting. The thought of my mother holding knitting needles is enough to make anyone who knows her laugh. There was one about the traditional architecture of the northern part of southeastern West Virginia. There was one huge old book that was so dusty that I couldn't even read the title. And that was just the beginning.

I dumped all three boxes upside down onto the carpet and scattered the books out across the floor so I could at least arrange them by size. They covered the carpet until I was walking on them like stepping stones, so I took off my shoes. At first, I was careful about the sizes, and made them look neat. Then I just shoved them into the shelves any way I could make them fit.

All the lower shelves were crammed full when I finally stepped back. It didn't look too bad. It probably wouldn't actually embarrass me until I made some new friends who came over and noticed the titles. If I ever made any new friends.

I took one more step backward, and my heel came down on the corner of something hard. It really hurt and I hopped around for a minute, trying not to scream. Then I saw what I had stepped on.

It was the huge book that was so dusty I hadn't been able to read the title. I picked it up and held it, still looking at the shelves. It weighed a ton and it was so big that it wouldn't fit on any of the lower shelves at all. I didn't want to put it up with my books. Maybe I could just sneak it into the trash. My mother would never miss it. It was probably some old cookbook or something. I wiped at the cover with the palm of my hand and felt a funny tingle on my skin.

The title was in big fancy letters, with double lines and loops that curved into tiny spirals out at the ends. The letters were deep red, and the cover, under all that dust, felt like real leather. *The Mad Inventor's Handbook,* it said. I began to flip through the pages and it

10

took me about half a minute to forget about unpacking, Tillison School, and just about everything else. It was the most amazing book that I had ever seen in my whole life.

CHAPTER TWO

It was a book about inventions, mostly. Some of them were just plain unbelievable. On every page there were detailed, precise-looking diagrams and drawings. There were little tiny flea swatters made from parts of old watches, and automatic cookie jars that refilled themselves. There were instructions for building a submarine that transformed into a biplane in three minutes. There was just about anything you could imagine. Some of it was crazy, but a lot of the designs looked like they would work.

I smiled, then I grinned, then I laughed out loud. There were enough projects in this book to keep me busy for years. I kept thumbing through the pages until I came to the last section. The last section was about magic. Really. There were strange spells and weird chants and stuff. There was an entire chapter about how to make a monster that would actually come to life. You had to have a real skeleton and some real hair and a bunch of other stuff. There were drawings of the magical hand signs and instructions on how to say the magic chants, and the book said there had to be a full moon. I whispered one of the chants a few times. The words were pretty, almost like music. Or poetry.

The odd tingle in my hands started again. It felt like when you sleep in a funny position and your hands go numb, then get all prickly when you move. It almost hurt. I closed the book and a little puff of dust rose from the pages. It was an *old* book, but, except for the dust, the pages looked new.

I looked at my hands. Maybe someone had sprayed the book with something that irritated your skin. Some bug spray or preservative or something. I was still smiling. It was going to be fun to try to make some of the designs. But that last section with all that crazy magic stuff was just incredible!

"How are you doing, Matt?" my mother called down the hall.

I put the book on the highest shelf and went down the hall into her room, feeling wonderful. She was trying to fit a bunch of old computer components into her closet. I recognized some of the stuff. There was one set of computer expansion boards we have moved at least three times. And an old monitor that, as far as I know, never worked. I smiled. I was feeling better than I had in weeks. My mom jumped backward when the monitor slipped out of her hands and clunked to the floor.

I smiled wider. "We could throw some of it away."

She frowned. When I tease my mom, she doesn't always get it. "I'll fit it all in somewhere," she said, looking around at me. Then she looked at me closely. I tried to stop smiling but I couldn't. "Matt? Are you up to something? Did you get all the books put away?"

I nodded. For a second I thought about telling her about *The Mad Inventor's Handbook,* then I decided

13

not to. No sense in worrying her about projects I might want to try.

"Why don't you start taking these down to the trash, Matt," she said, waving at the piles of empty boxes on the floor. "It's down in the parking area. I'll start on the kitchen."

I looked at the empty boxes. There were more in my room. It would take a few trips, which sounded like more fun than unpacking silverware, so I didn't complain. I loaded up and headed for the door. The boxes were stacked so high that I couldn't see where I was going, but I made it down the hall.

At the elevator, I jammed the boxes between my stomach and the wall and felt around until I hit the button. When I heard the elevator doors open, I maneuvered forward slowly. The boxes hit something.

"Hey, watch out!"

I couldn't see anybody, but it was a kid's voice. I backed up a little and wrestled the boxes around until I could see him. He was sitting on the floor reading a book. He looked a little younger than me, maybe ten or eleven. He had thick glasses and curly brown hair.

"I'm sorry," I said. I tried to see the title of his book. You can tell a lot about people from what they read. But the boxes were so awkward that I gave up. Besides, he had already looked down, turned a page, and was ignoring me completely.

I wrenched back around, trying to hit the lobby button with the corner of one of the boxes. Then I tried freeing one hand. The boxes tipped and I got my hand back, fast. The kid ignored me completely. I turned sideways again and tried to bend over far enough to hit the button with my forehead. The kid turned another page. It took three tries before I managed to press the button down hard enough, and it hurt my forehead. The elevator doors closed and we started down. The kid turned another page, acting like I wasn't there at all. He made me furious.

"Do you live here?" I asked with my teeth clenched. I sounded like I was about to hit him. That got his attention.

He looked up and blinked like an owl. "No," he said with a perfectly straight face. "I'm an alien. From Tethys. But I just *love* your elevators here on earth. So once in a while I come down and take a ride. Tethys is a moon of—"

"I know what Tethys is," I snapped at him.

He grinned, and I got a good look at his braces. There was enough metal in his mouth to construct a bridge. A long bridge. I also got a glimpse of the book cover. It was a science fiction book I recognized, about these aliens who get stuck in the event horizon of a black hole in space and time stops for them.

"I bet you really don't know what Tethys is," he said quietly. He was still grinning up at me. So he thought he was smart because he knew a little about astronomy? Well, he had picked the wrong kid to be a jerk to. I looked straight at him and smiled sweetly.

"I've read that book. Do you understand about the Schwarzschild radius?"

His grin faded. "Uh . . . well. I . . . not all of it."

"Maybe I'll explain it to you sometime," I said as the elevator came to a stop. I turned a clumsy half circle and stepped out. "But you might not be able to understand," I added, looking back over my shoulder. Then I walked away.

"Anybody ever tell you that acting like a genius is obnoxious?" the kid yelled behind me.

I whirled around, and one of the smaller boxes came loose and sailed across the floor. The kid was standing up, holding the elevator doors open.

"People have told me that all my life," I told him honestly.

He nodded, but he really wasn't looking at me. "Yeah. Me too," he said. He moved back and the elevator doors slid shut, missing his nose by about a quarter of an inch. He didn't even blink. He must have practiced for hours to be able to do that. I went through the lobby into the parking area and dumped the boxes. On my way back up, the kid was still there.

"My name is Matt Jameson," I said as I got in.

"Big deal," he said without looking up.

Furious, I pushed the second floor button. When I got off, I saw Mr. Norris walking down the hall toward me.

"You're not playing in the elevator are you?" he called.

I shook my head. "I'm taking trash down."

He came up to me. "Good. Playing in the elevators is strictly against the rules." He was staring at me with his eyebrows all hunched up and his mouth tight and grumpy. I nodded as I turned away, remembering what my mother had said about staying on his good side. It wasn't going to be easy. Between him and the elevator kid, I was feeling lousy again.

When I got back, my mother had another load of empty boxes ready. So I gathered them up and headed back toward the elevator. Mr. Norris was gone. I was sort of hoping that the kid would still be in the elevator, but he was gone, too. I went up and down three or four more times. On the last load, someone had closed the door that led into the parking area. I was

16

trying to open it without setting down the boxes when I heard someone sneeze right behind me. I whirled around, startled.

There was a very strange-looking woman standing there. She was kind of old but she was wearing denim shorts and a backpack, and her hair hung down in thick silver braids. Her eyes were bright blue, and she had those neat wrinkles that fanned out from her eyes. My mother calls them laugh lines. She was staring at me. She sneezed again, and for a second she looked puzzled or confused or something.

"Oh," she said softly. "Oh, I see." She shook her head. "I think, young lady, that you should be at home doing some very important reading."

I was trying to figure out what she was talking about when she smiled widely and nodded. "I apologize. Of course you don't know about it yet. But you will. Oh my, how exciting. But first things first. My name is Mrs. Hannover. Are you moving in?"

Her voice was beautiful, as if she was almost singing the words. I nodded and introduced myself. She shook my hand when I stuck it out from under the boxes.

"Lovely. We need more young people," she said, and her eyes twinkled. "Besides, that old stinker Mr. Norris isn't happy unless he can get upset about something. You are going to make him *very* happy." She sneezed, then rubbed at her nose with a lacy handkerchief.

I started laughing. I couldn't help it. "Is he always that grumpy?" I asked. "All he ever talks about is his rules."

She nodded and pushed the heavy door open. "Rules are very important to Mr. Norris." She waited

17

while I took the boxes out. As I came back, she sneezed again. "Do let me know when you get started. Perhaps I can be of help to you." I nodded politely, because she seemed nice and I didn't want to offend her, but I had no idea what she was talking about. She got into a little green sports car and waved good-bye merrily. I waved back, wondering if everyone in this building was going to be either strange or grumpy.

My father got home and helped us finish unpacking. Then we all collapsed into bed early. First thing the next morning, Dad got a call from the University of Mexico.

My father is a pretty famous archaeologist and he's always getting calls like that. Usually they just want advice about how to preserve an artifact that they've found in a ruin somewhere or something. Sometimes, though, they want more than that. This was one of those calls. The Mexican government had just found the ruins of an unusual Mayan temple in a jungle in the Yucatán, and they wanted him to help them begin the dig.

Archaeologists call it that—a "dig." That's exactly what it is. They dig and dig and dig and try to find things that people from a long time ago left behind. My dad loves it. He says it's like a treasure hunt, except you find knowledge about the past instead of gold. My dad talks like that. He's fun to listen to.

He sat me down to explain why he was going to be gone for a while. He always sits down with me, just the two of us, before he goes anywhere. I kind of like it—even though it makes me feel like a little kid again. My father has brown eyes and when he feels bad about something, they get all big and solemn. He hugged me for a long time, then started talking about the dig in

18

Mexico. I could tell he was excited. But he also felt bad.

"I'm sorry I won't be here when you start school, Matt," he told me. "But you can tell me about Tillison when I get back. I know you're going to be fine."

In a way I was upset. I was pretty nervous about going to the new school, and Dad usually understands stuff like that better than Mom. But I could tell he really wanted to go, and it seemed kind of dumb to argue and get him all upset too. So I just hugged him harder and I helped him pack. The next morning, my mother and I took him to the airport. I promised to write him a lot, and he promised to write back.

When we got home, I spent some time setting up my computer and fiddling around with a program I was working on. Then the doorbell rang. It was the elevator kid. He came in and looked around, smiling exactly *once,* when my mom said hello. She asked him if he lived in the building. He nodded. Then she asked him if he had met me. He nodded again. After a minute of trying to get him to talk, Mom gave up and went back in the kitchen. I could hear her banging around, getting things organized. The elevator kid just sat down on the couch. Finally he looked at me.

"The people who lived here before you had to move because they tried to keep a stray dog they found in the park. Mean old Mr. Norris just kicked them right out. Weird, huh?"

I didn't know whether he meant they were weird for wanting the dog, or whether it was weird that Mr. Norris made them move. So I decided not to answer him. *He* was pretty weird himself. He just sat there, staring at nothing. I finally asked him his name.

"Eddie. Eddie Meyer," he told me. "Mr. Norris

19

yelled at me for reading in the elevator this morning. He made a new rule, just for me. No reading in the elevators. Have you met him yet? He's pretty weird.''

''It seems like rules are about the only thing he cares about,'' I agreed. Eddie was now looking at a place on the ceiling that didn't look any different from the rest of it. ''What grade are you in?'' I asked him.

He frowned and didn't say anything for a minute. Then he looked straight at me, and his voice sounded like he was daring me to start an argument. ''I go to a school where they don't really have grades.''

I swallowed. ''Tillison?''

He nodded, his eyes wide behind his thick glasses. ''How'd you know? Most kids have never heard of it.''

''I start there this year,'' I told him. I waited but he didn't say anything else, so I had to ask him. ''What's it like, Eddie?''

He took off his glasses and rubbed them on his shirt. ''It's okay, mostly. And kind of weird, too. Is your mom going to drive you every day? Or are you going to be walking?''

I thought about it. It was only a few blocks. ''Walking, probably. My mother is always pretty rushed in the morning.''

He looked over my shoulder, then at the ceiling, then at the floor. ''Mine too,'' he said. ''We may as well walk together.''

I wasn't sure I wanted to walk to school with Eddie Meyer. On the other hand, going alone might be worse. I needed time to think about it. So I tried to distract him. ''Want to look at my books or something?''

He didn't answer. He was looking at the ceiling again. ''I have a book that might clear up the

Schwarzschild radius for you,'' I said, standing up, trying to get his attention.

He stood up without saying anything at all and followed me down the hall. When he saw the bookshelves he whistled. Then he got closer and started reading titles. His face squinched up and he looked at me. ''What *are* all these weird books?''

I blushed, which always makes me mad at myself. ''A lot of them are my mother's books,'' I said. ''She likes old books.''

Eddie grinned. ''She must. These are really weird.''

That did it. I was angry. ''Do you know how much you use that word?'' I demanded.

He stared at me. ''What word?''

''Weird.''

''Maybe I like it.'' He was stretching up and scanning the titles of my books now. ''You like dogs or something? You sure have a lot of weird little kid's books about dogs.''

''I've always wanted a dog. I still do.'' I said it too loudly, but I was not about to let weird Eddie Meyer embarrass me again.

He rubbed his cheek. ''Weird. I never understood why girls get all mushy over dogs. I mean, dogs are neat, but it's weird how—''

''Here,'' I said, to shut him up. ''The Schwarzschild radius is explained in this one.'' I pulled down one of my astronomy books and started flipping pages, but he wasn't looking.

''Hey, what's this?'' He reached past me and pulled at *The Mad Inventor's Handbook*. I flinched. I did *not* want him looking at that book. ''That's weird,'' he said in a puzzled voice. ''It won't come out.'' He reached up again.

21

I didn't think about what to do. I just did it. "Leave that one alone," I yelled, grabbing his arm and jerking it down.

Eddie frowned at me, his eyes narrow and squinty behind the thick glasses. "Sure thing. You don't have to break my arm. You're pretty weird, you know that? I wouldn't have even come up here except that Mrs. Hannover said I should."

I remembered the odd, friendly woman who had held the door open for me. "You know Mrs. Hannover?"

Eddie nodded. "Yeah. She's pretty weird, but she's nice."

That did it. If I had to hear the word *weird* one more time, I knew I would throw up. I shoved the astronomy book into his chest and he clutched at it. "Here," I said abruptly. "Third chapter. You can bring it back when you're done." Then I went and stood by the door until he walked back into the hall. I just wanted him to go home. I was lonely, but Eddie Meyer was a hard kid to like.

I heard voices in the living room. Eddie nodded. "That's my mother. She said she might be coming up to meet your parents."

We went into the living room. My mother was explaining that my dad was in Mexico. She introduced me to Eddie's mother. Mrs. Meyer smiled and they both said all the nice friendly things about me and Eddie that mothers always say when they meet someone else's kid. They discovered that we were both going to Tillison and talked about how nice that was. Eddie made a face at me as they left. His braces sparkled.

My mother smiled brightly after they were gone.

"Matt, that's really lucky, finding someone who goes to Tillison. Eddie can show you around and help you make friends."

I tried to smile. I could tell she was really glad that I had met someone from Tillison. But I wasn't exactly thrilled about having Eddie Meyer in my life.

Mom went back into the kitchen and I could hear her arranging cupboards. We were almost unpacked, but not quite. I knew I should go help, but I tiptoed down the hall instead.

My hands tingled a little when I pulled *The Mad Inventor's Handbook* down off the shelf, but I ignored it. Whatever caused it didn't seem to hurt or get worse or anything. If Eddie was all there was available in the new friends department, it was going to be a lonely year. A new school where I didn't know anybody except Eddie Meyer, and another landlord who wouldn't let me have a dog. I was going to need a really interesting project to keep myself busy.

I flopped down on my bed and started turning pages. Suddenly, an idea came into my mind from nowhere at all. It was completely crazy, and I knew it, but I turned to the last section of the book anyway. I read through the chants and magic spells. After a while I was taking notes and making experimental changes here and there in the directions. When my mother called me for dinner, I hid my notebook.

CHAPTER THREE

One morning I ran into Mr. Norris in the elevator. He looked as grumpy as always, but I tried to be polite. "Hello, Mr. Norris," I said.

"On your way to school?" he asked. I guess he liked the idea of school starting. He sounded hopeful. He probably figured that school kept kids out of trouble or something.

I shook my head. "No. School hasn't started yet. I'm on my way to that little grocery on the corner. Mom needs some noodles." It sounded silly but it was true. Mr. Norris was still looking at me but he made me so nervous I couldn't think of anything else to say.

We both got out at the lobby and I walked toward the double glass doors that led on to the street. Mr. Norris was right behind me. I stopped and held the door open for him. He went through without saying thank you or anything. We had barely taken two steps onto the sidewalk when Mrs. Hannover came pedaling up on a bicycle.

"Good morning," she sang out, smiling at me. Then she nodded at Mr. Norris. He frowned at both of us. Mrs. Hannover smiled sweetly at him. "Beautiful morning, isn't it, Mr. Norris?" He sort of nodded but he didn't answer her.

"My mother needs some noodles," I said, edging past them. I just wanted to get away from Mr. Norris. A car honked and I looked up. A pretty black dog was running across the street. Another car honked and braked hard and for a second I thought the dog was going to get hit—but he made it. Across the street a woman was watching, her hands over her mouth. The dog dashed up to us, panting and wagging his tail. Mr. Norris waved his arms. "Get away," he shouted. "Go on!"

The dog jumped back toward the traffic. A passing car swerved away from the curb and honked. The dog was startled into standing still for an instant. I lunged forward and caught his collar. He was scared and tried to get away but I held on, talking to him, telling him to take it easy. After he calmed down he licked at my hand. Mrs. Hannover leaned her bike against the building and came over to scratch his ears.

"Such a lovely dog you are," she told him. Then she sneezed, and looked at me strangely. "Mathilda, before you—" she began, but Mr. Norris interrupted her.

"Don't get any ideas about bringing that animal into the building, Mathilda," he said sternly. "You know the rules."

Mrs. Hannover sneezed loudly. My hands started tingling. I looked up, feeling very confused. The woman who had been watching crossed the street and rushed toward us. She looked pale and kept thanking us over and over again for saving her dog. You could tell she really loved him, and he jumped up and down wagging like crazy. Finally, she led him away, scolding him softly for running into the street. Mr. Norris was still standing there, frowning as usual. Mrs. Han-

25

nover sneezed. I started to wonder if she was allergic to dogs. Or maybe I was. My hands were still tingly.

"I'll never understand why people like dogs," Mr. Norris said, scowling. His eyebrows were bunched together like he had a headache or something.

"Well, I do," I said, suddenly feeling too angry to keep my mouth shut. "I like dogs a lot. I've always wanted one. And just because you don't like them doesn't give you the right to scare a dog out into the traffic like that. He could have been killed."

Mr. Norris shook his head. "You just remember the rules, young lady, and don't get any ideas about trying to sneak a stray dog into the building. I've already had to evict one family for that."

"How could I forget the rules?" I practically yelled at him. "You never talk about anything else." My hands were still tingling and I felt strange.

"Do I have to speak to your mother about your behavior?" he asked in a low, tense voice. I glanced at Mrs. Hannover. She was sneezing. I started to walk away. I just wanted to get out of there.

"Don't wash your jacket until you think about it, Mathilda," Mrs. Hannover called after me. She sneezed again. I pretended I hadn't heard her and walked faster. I felt like saying something *really* rude to Mr. Norris. No matter how polite I tried to be, he was mean. And he could have killed that dog, shooing him into the street like that.

It took me two blocks to calm down. Then, just in front of the little grocery store, I stopped and thought about what Mrs. Hannover had said. I stood very still and raised my hands. There were three long black dog hairs stuck to the cuff of my jacket.

The Mad Inventor's Handbook had said you needed a

26

real skeleton and a few strands of real hair and some other stuff. But how could Mrs. Hannover possibly know about that? I found a tissue in my pocket and wrapped the hair in it. I put the tissue in my pocket. Then I tried hard not to think about anything but noodles.

When I got home I decided that enough was enough. I had a new school to worry over and Mr. Norris might be upset enough to talk to my mother. I had more problems than I needed already. I almost threw *The Mad Inventor's Handbook* away, but as soon as I touched it my hands started to tingle. I jerked my hands back and sat down at my desk.

I wrote a letter to my dad and tried to sound normal, even though I wasn't feeling very normal. Later that night I put the tissue with the dog hair in it in a drawer, way at the back, under some sweaters. I promised myself I would forget about it.

The next couple of weeks went by fast. All of a sudden there were only two weeks left before school started. I had been exploring the neighborhood when my mother couldn't think of something for me to do. The park was pretty nice. There were always a lot of people jogging, and people with dogs, and people with little kids. On our block, there were a lot of little shops along the street.

One day my mother said I could go explore for an hour while she did errands. Coming out of the lobby, I saw Eddie standing on the sidewalk talking to Mrs. Hannover. She was wearing a long embroidered skirt and her braids hung down over a peasant blouse, like a Gypsy grandmother. She waved when she saw me coming.

I sort of waved back, but I didn't want to talk to

her. I mean, I was trying hard to forget about *The Mad Inventor's Handbook* and the dog hair wrapped in tissue under my sweaters. I didn't believe in magic. Every time I thought about all the crazy things that she had said, and all the strange ideas I had been getting, it made me nervous. So I turned and went into the first store that I could, hoping she and Eddie wouldn't follow me. It wasn't until I was inside that I realized what kind of store it was.

Taxidermy.

All kinds of dead stuffed animals.

Yuck. Double yuck. *Triple* yuck.

But I couldn't just turn and go back out. So I looked around. The whole place smelled icky. In the back, deer's heads were hung side by side high on the wall. Beneath them there was a sad-looking moose with dust on its antlers. There were owls and a couple of stuffed rabbits on little pedestals. After a minute I noticed a man behind the counter. He was sorting through something in a box, but he glanced up. "Can I help you?"

I looked back out through the windows. Eddie and Mrs. Hannover were still standing near the curb, talking. I turned toward a skeleton that had been mounted on a piece of polished wood as if it were standing up. The bones were wired together. "I'm just looking," I mumbled. The smell of the place was making me a little sick. More than a little.

"That's a coyote," the man was saying. "It's illegal to hunt them, but somebody hit that one with a car. A friend of mine saw it along the road and brought it to me." He was smiling. I moved away from the skeleton, but it didn't help. He kept talking.

"None of the bones was broken, so I set it up. I'm not sure why. I put it on the stand like that for fun."

28

Fun? I thought. But I nodded. If I could stand the smell in here a little longer, maybe Eddie and Mrs. Hannover would leave. I looked out the window and groaned silently. They were still there, talking. I turned back toward the skeleton and pretended to look at it. The bones were smooth and milk white. I touched it, barely. And my fingers tingled.

I must have made a noise because the man behind the counter stood up suddenly. "Are you all right, miss?"

I nodded, kept nodding . . . I couldn't seem to *stop* nodding. I was not, in any sense of the words, all right. My brain was working so fast that it was making me dizzy. My hand was still tingling a little. I was staring at the skeleton. "How much do you want for it?" I heard myself say hoarsely. My fingers closed around my wallet in my pocket. I had five dollars left from my birthday money from my dad.

The man was looking at me strangely, and I couldn't blame him a bit. I was shaking with excitement. Or with something. All I knew was that I had to have that coyote skeleton and I had to get out of that shop before I got sick. The man shifted around and fiddled with a ballpoint pen. After what seemed like a hundred years he looked at me and said, "Five dollars?"

He said it like it was a question, and he was really staring at me. I guess I didn't look like someone who would buy a coyote skeleton. But then, I couldn't imagine what someone who would buy one *would* look like. "Five dollars is fine," I told him. But he acted like he hadn't heard me.

"Or four dollars would be all right."

"Great," I said quickly. I just wanted to get out of there. I was feeling absolutely strange. But he was still talking.

"Or three dollars, really," he said with a smile. "I just did it for fun. I just kept thinking that someone would want it."

"Three dollars is perfect," I cut him off. "Can you . . . could you put it in a box or something?"

He nodded. "Sure. It isn't glued, I just did it for fun, like I said. Is this for a school project or something?" He smiled again, his whole face lighting up. "Hey! I bet you go to that genius school over on Maple Street? Tillison, isn't it?"

I shook my head, then nodded, then shook it again. He was looking at me like I was a perfect specimen of *Girlus Nutsus*. Probably I was. But the last thing I wanted to do was talk to him. I needed to get out into the fresh air and think. Or stop thinking. Or something.

He brought a box and started to pack the skeleton into it slowly and carefully, taking the wires out in a few places to make it fit. I stood still, afraid to touch it again, afraid my hand would tingle. I just wanted to get it home, and then—and then I didn't know what. I glanced out the window. Eddie and Mrs. Hannover had gone. Good. The skeleton was almost in the box. I paid the man and tried to smile a little, but my smile must have looked strange because he just shook his head.

When I finally got outside, the sunlight seemed too bright and the whole street looked unfamiliar and odd. But the fresh air began to clear my head, and by the time I pushed against the lobby doors and started for the elevator, I was feeling better. I would just put the skeleton in my closet. Maybe I *would* use it for a biology project or something.

"Won't you join Eddie and me for tea?"

It was Mrs. Hannover's voice.

30

I whirled around, too fast. The coyote skeleton rattled in the box. I instantly felt shaky again and I couldn't get my mouth working. "Oh—ah," I stammered. "Oh, well. Thank you but I . . ."

"Nonsense," she said. "Yes, you can. I have been wanting to talk to you before you get started." She sneezed into a tissue. "Or am I already too late?"

I stared at her. Half of what she said made sense. The other half seemed like she was reading my mind, but my mind, just then, was not making sense at all. She took my arm firmly. I tried to pull away, but she patted my shoulder and kept talking.

"Mathilda, you will enjoy this tea. It's tamarindo. You know what that is—from the seedpods of a tree that grows in the Yucatán. The Mayan Indians used it as a medicine for fever. You've never been to my apartment and I would like to talk to you about what you are thinking of trying to think about trying."

My brain began to spin in circles. I *did* know what tamarindo was, from a book about the Mayan Indians that my father had gotten me. And I was certainly thinking of trying to think about trying something. I rubbed one hand across my eyes. Mrs. Hannover was still talking. I wasn't really listening, but somehow she had gotten me moving.

She steered me away from the elevators and through a door I had never noticed. We went down some steep stairs and turned into a narrow hallway.

"This was the maid's quarters," she was saying, "back when the building was one huge house. This is an old building, you know. Older than I am." She laughed softly and opened a door.

Eddie was sitting on a mahogany-colored rug that covered half the floor. There were plants along the

31

walls. In fact, it was hard to *see* the walls, there were so many plants. A few were tall and straight with shiny, broad leaves, but most of them were ferns. It was like standing in a clearing in a rain forest. Mrs. Hannover pushed me gently and I went in, clutching the box. I stumbled over the edge of the rug and the skeleton made a funny clinking sound. My stomach clenched.

"What's in there?" Eddie asked, pointing at the box.

"I . . . ah . . . well, I . . ." My mouth still wasn't working. Or my brain. I turned around and headed toward the door. Mrs. Hannover took my arm. We swung around like we were square dancing.

"Sit down, Mathilda. Sit down. And Eddie," she said, turning to look at him, "I want you to leave Mathilda alone."

"Matt," I said automatically. "My name is Matt."

Mrs. Hannover smiled gently and patted my arm. Then she disappeared through the ferns. I couldn't see where she had gone.

"What's in the box?" Eddie whispered. I didn't answer him. A second later Mrs. Hannover was back with a tray that held a steaming pot of tea and three cups. She set it on a table I hadn't noticed.

The table had been made from dark wood. It was low and there were carvings all over it. Eddie sat down by the table, cross-legged on the floor. Mrs. Hannover sort of pulled and pushed me until I sat next to him, holding the box tightly on my lap. The tea smelled like apricot jam as she poured it.

Eddie leaned closer. "Mrs. Hannover says I'm supposed to help you with something," he whispered. I moved away from him. Mrs. Hannover was smiling at

32

me in a patient way. I bent awkwardly over the box in my lap and sipped the tea. It was good.

"Now, then," Mrs. Hannover said. "Don't you feel better?" I nodded. I did feel a little better. I wasn't sure why, but I did. I looked around, noticing something different every second. There were bright-colored African masks hanging on the walls, peeking through the leaves of the tallest ferns. The couch was half covered with drooping fern fronds. On a small table by the couch there were small clay statues of the Egyptian gods.

"You'd really like my father," I blurted out. "He's an archaeologist and he really likes this kind of junk— I mean stuff," I corrected myself quickly, waving one hand at the room.

"I'm sure that I will like him," she said, smiling. I sipped the tea and tried to calm down a little. Mrs. Hannover's whole apartment was interesting. The tea table had a glass top. I bent forward to look. Under the glass, a whole fantasy story had been carved into the dark wood. There were knights and dragons fighting, and unicorns leaping around them. The table was set on a second rug. It wasn't woven like the bigger one, but made of some kind of natural animal skin. I ran my fingers over the soft, deep fur. It was cream colored and curly. For a second I just enjoyed the soft feeling. Then my hands began to tingle.

"Eddie tells me that you will be going to Tillison School this year, too," Mrs Hannover was saying in a friendly voice.

I gulped and nodded, and raised my hands to grip the edge of the carved table. The box jammed into my stomach. The tingling stopped. "Y-yes," I managed to murmur. "Tillison. Yes."

Mrs. Hannover smiled. "You will like Tillison School, Mathilda."

"My name is Matt," I said, automatically. Mrs. Hannover looked at me steadily and her blue eyes seemed to get cloudy.

"Why are you ashamed of your name? Mathilda is a grand, brave name. Do you know what it means?"

I felt dizzy. Too much was happening. Here was this nice old lady talking about my name while I sat with a box of bones on my lap and drank Mayan tamarindo tea. And why were my hands tingling all the time? It was getting hard to think straight. "I . . . I . . . no," I stammered.

Mrs. Hannover smiled. "It means that you are brave. Not only brave, but determined. Mathilda. Mah . . . til . . . da!" She said it like it was a beautiful piece of music or something. "It means that you will be brave and try hard to accomplish what you set out to do."

I looked past Mrs. Hannover at the ferns behind her. I had never liked my name, no matter what it meant. I took another sip of tea, trying to calm down. As I set the cup down again, my hand slipped. The tea spilled, splattering the glass tabletop and the woolly rug. I snatched up a napkin and bent over the box on my lap, rubbing at the rug. My hand immediately began to tingle again. I jerked my hand away and the skeleton in the box rattled. I stammered an apology, blushing. Eddie stared at me.

"Don't worry about the rug," Mrs. Hannover said softly. "It's a sheepskin from New Zealand; it won't stain." She smiled and rubbed her nose. Then she sneezed, and stared at me. "Oh," she said. "Oh, I see."

For a second, I was sure that she knew all about the crazy ideas I had been having. It didn't make sense, but what else had made sense lately? "Look . . . I do ah, I do have to go now," I said desperately. I stood up awkwardly, clutching at the box, and moved toward the door.

"You're really acting weird, Mathilda," Eddie said.

I blushed again, but I didn't stop moving. "I do, I really do, I have to go now. I have to go now." I clenched my teeth to keep myself from repeating it again. I sounded like the recording on the phone that tells you what time it is. Eddie grimaced and his braces glinted at me. Mrs. Hannover just nodded politely. I gripped the box so hard that my knuckles went white. Then I turned and ran out the door.

I made it up the stairs and into the elevator before I realized I was holding my breath. I was just letting it out when Mr. Norris got into the elevator with me. I hunched around the box, terrified that he would talk to me. How could I sound normal? Or even close?

"Does your mother know where you are?" he asked, frowning. "I discourage parents in the building from leaving their children unsupervised." He was staring at me. His eyes were the color of the sky on a cloudy, windy, nasty, cold day. I nodded and looked away. "She does know where you are?" Mr. Norris asked again.

I bit the inside of my lip. I was still mad at him for almost scaring that black dog back into the street. And I was sick of him acting like I was a criminal or something. But if I said anything, he'd tell my mother for sure—and he would start keeping even more of an eye on me. I didn't need that. At all. Not now. Especially not now.

Finally, the elevator doors opened again and I ran

down the hall. "No running in the hallways, Mathilda," Mr. Norris yelled from behind me. "That's a rule here."

I forced myself to walk. At the door, I shifted the box to one side and searched my pockets. My hands were shaking a little. I could feel Mr. Norris staring at me. For a second, I was sure that I had forgotten my key, and that I would have to turn around and ask Mr. Norris to let me in with his passkey. I felt like screaming, but then I found the key in my back pocket.

When I got inside our apartment, my mother called out, "Hello, Matt."

I swallowed. She had gotten back from her errands? Where would I hide the box? What I would say if she came out and asked me what was in it?

"Did you find any interesting shops?" my mother called. "I'll be right out, I'm just changing clothes."

I sprinted down the hall and shoved the box into my closet as far back against the wall as it would go. By the time my mother came out of her room, I was smiling. Sort of anyway. I talked to her and tried to sound like everything was just regular, average, unremarkable, and peachy. I told her about a knitting shop I had seen a week before. Then I tried, hard, not to think about old magic books, dog hair, and coyote skeletons. I tried to forget about the whole thing.

CHAPTER FOUR

I was almost glad when the first day of school finally came. I had rearranged my room ten times, and I had finished a computer program I was working on before we moved. I had started some reading that would help with classes at school. I had even cleaned the bathroom twice, without my mother asking me. I was helping with dinner almost every night. My mother was beginning to think something was wrong with me. There was, of course, but I sure couldn't tell her about *The Mad Inventor's Handbook* or the box of coyote bones in my closet.

I had even spent time with Eddie, trading science fiction books and letting him use my computer. Afternoons with Eddie weren't always terrific, but he wasn't bad if you just ignored about half of what he said. Or maybe more like two-thirds. I was running out of ways to keep busy.

So when the alarm went off and I remembered that it was the first day of school, I only felt crummy for a minute or two. Anything was starting to sound better than another day of Eddie Meyer saying "weird" about everything.

Mom hugged me good-bye. "Have fun, honey. I think you're going to like it."

I nodded, feeling a little numb and wishing my dad was there. He would have walked with me, or told me a story about once when he went to a new school. But my mom was smiling cheerfully at me so I smiled back.

Eddie and I met in the lobby at seven-thirty. He was almost nice, but maybe he just wasn't awake enough to be his usual uncharming self. We went across the park, walking along without talking. Eddie knew a couple of shortcuts through the trees, and within five minutes we were standing on the old stone steps of Tillison School.

At the curb, car after car was pulling up, and kids got out and walked toward the school. There were about two hundred students, my mother had told me. That was much smaller than the other schools I had been to, but right now, with everybody milling around on the sidewalk and no familiar faces, it felt bigger. My mouth was dry.

Eddie and I went up the steps. A lot of kids said hello to him. He didn't answer, but nobody seemed upset or surprised. And of course, he didn't introduce me to anyone. Just inside the doors, he pointed at a big chart hung on a bulletin board.

"Class assignments. We have to find out where we're supposed to go." I nodded and we moved into the crowd around the bulletin board. Kids were making the usual noises. You know what I mean. Somebody got a teacher he didn't like, somebody else ended up in a different class from her best friend. Kids were groaning and giggling and shuffling their notebooks, then weaving their way out of the crowd toward class.

It wasn't too long before Eddie and I were right up front. I saw my name.

MATHILDA JAMESON, HOMEROOM 12, JACK DANNERS

"Do you know Mr. Danners?" I whispered as we worked our way back through the crowd of kids.

Eddie nodded without saying anything at all. I felt like strangling him. Why couldn't he ever just be nice to me? "Eddie, what's Mr. Danners *like?*" I whispered.

Eddie looked around, sort of focusing on outer space, like he always did. I could never tell if he had heard me or not. Finally his eyes snapped into focus and he grinned his metallic, un-nice grin.

"They give Danners all the weirdos. You'll fit right in."

I really thought I might hit him for a second. I mean, I was used to him being a jerk like that, but I was nervous and this time it upset me. Eddie actually noticed. For a second I thought he was going to apologize. Which would probably have made me faint.

"You'll like him, Matt," he said quietly. "You will. He's good, especially with computer stuff. You'll have Danners for science and math and computers, and somebody else for English and social studies. He'll tell you who the other teacher is today."

I didn't quite know how to handle the fact that Eddie Meyer was being almost nice to me. Maybe it was a mistake or something. I looked at him hard, but he was focusing on outer space again.

I glanced around. The crowd was thinning out. "How do I get to room twelve?"

"That way," Eddie said, sort of pointing with his

39

chin. "There's only two stories. Ten rooms upstairs and ten down. Just go up the stairs." Then, before I could say anything else, he walked away.

I passed through groups of kids who were talking and went up the stairs. The whole building felt like a museum. The floors were polished wood, the walls were spotless white, and the ceilings were high. Voices echoed. At the top of the stairs, I hugged my notebook and took a deep breath. The hall was *wide*.

I walked slowly, looking into the numbered rooms as I went by. It was sure different from the schools I was used to. There were computers in almost every room, and the desks were in half circles or arranged around lab tables. In one room there weren't any desks at all, just mats like you use in gym class. There were kids sitting in pairs and threesomes, talking and laughing. The rooms were big, but there weren't many kids in each one. My mother had said the classes would be smaller. That was supposed to be one of the advantages of Tillison. More teachers for fewer kids. I figured it out. Eddie had said ten rooms upstairs and ten down. Twenty rooms for two hundred kids. Ten kids in a class? That was going to be strange.

I hesitated outside room twelve. It looked like a regular classroom—except for the desks in a half circle and the computers lined up at the back of the room—and the fact that compared to the schoolrooms I was used to, it seemed empty.

I walked in slowly. Mr. Danners was at the back of the room, talking to a girl with long dark hair and funny clothes. He was tall, with a beard. He was wearing jeans and a denim shirt with a tie. He and the girl were laughing about something. She had on a deep purple dress that kind of wrapped around her waist

40

and up over one shoulder. There were little gold threads woven through the cloth.

Mr. Danners looked up and made a waving motion with his hand that seemed to say I could sit anywhere I wanted to. Some kids were already sitting down. The girl talking to Mr. Danners wasn't the only one who wore odd clothes. There were two boys wearing suits and ties, and one who had spiky blue hair and wore a torn sweatshirt. The girls were even more interesting. They wore anything and everything, it looked like. I realized something, and at first it made me uncomfortable. Then it made me feel good.

Almost all these kids were different somehow. They probably all had brains that worked overtime and got them into trouble. Or they wouldn't be here.

I sat down at a desk and looked around. A girl plopped into the seat next to mine, slapping her notebook down on the desk hard enough to make me flinch. She had on jeans and a western shirt and a red bandana around her neck. She looked at me.

"Are you new? You must be." For a second, I just stared at her. She had an accent like a cowboy in an old movie. She said "you" in two syllables, like "yee-oo," and new was "nee-oo."

I nodded. I put out my hand. "My name's Matt Jameson."

She just smiled and shook hands and didn't make any comment about my name.

"I'm Grady. Pam Grady," she said, pronouncing it Pay-am Grai-dee. "But everybody just calls me Grady."

I smiled at her. "What's Mr. Danners like?"

Grady fiddled with her notebook. "Well, people say he's hard. Really hard. Kids like him, though."

She leaned forward in her chair. "I wonder who we're going to have for English and social studies. Has he said?"

I shook my head. "Not yet. He's been talking to that girl."

"Oh." Grady said, twisting around to see. "That's Shernoz. She's Indian. She's really hot on computers. She's kind of shy, but she can be fun, too."

I started to ask her about some of the other kids, but Mr. Danners came to the front of the room and waited until we all quieted down. "Hi," he said, smiling. "Summer short enough for you?" Everybody moaned and made noises at him.

"Summer is *never* long enough," Grady said loudly. The kids made even more noise for a second, then quieted down again.

"Okay, okay," Mr. Danners said, smiling. "You've got me for computers, math, and science, and Gayle Webster for the rest." He looked around the room. "I know most of you, don't I?" He nodded toward me. "We've got a couple new kids this year. Mathilda Jameson, right?"

I took a deep breath. "I prefer to be called Matt," I said as evenly as I could. I was blushing and thinking about what Mrs. Hannover had said about my name. More than that I was waiting for someone to tease me or for Mr. Danners to say that calling me Matt would be confusing because it was usually a boy's name or that there was another Matt who was a boy in the class or something. But he didn't.

"Fine," Mr. Danners said. "Matt it is. And one more—" he nodded toward a boy who had been sitting silently in a desk near the door. "Devin Yen, right?" The boy nodded.

42

"The rest of you," Mr. Danners said, looking around the room, "introduce yourselves to Devin and Matt as the day goes on, will you? Be polite for once and all that." Then he pointed toward the computers at the back of the room and smiled. "Rise, kiddos, and shine. We have a lot of interesting work to do. Let's hit it."

Everybody stood up and moved to the back of the room. The computers were new . . . not five-year-old junkers like we had had at my old school, and I realized after a second that we each had one. No taking turns. I sat down and flipped through the disks. Some of them were familiar. "Boot up," Mr. Danners told us. I got the computer up and running and then looked up. Mr. Danners was pacing back and forth in front of us. He started talking.

Three hours later I was almost in shock. Mr. Danners knew things about computers that I had never even heard of. And he loved questions. You know how some teachers hate it when you tell them you don't understand something? Or they make you feel like you've done something wrong? Mr. Danners acted like you had just handed him an ice cream cone.

"Shernoz," he would say, "that's a beautiful question. A *wonderful* question. Anybody know? No? Let's think . . . a program built to respond in a random way? Does random become patterned eventually? There are scientists all over the world working with this kind of stuff. What do you think, people?" And we would try to figure it out.

But the most exciting thing he said came when he said good-bye to us at the end of class. "Tomorrow I want to start talking about what the entire computer industry is always talking about," he said. "About the

43

creation of real intelligence in a computer. I personally am not sure that it's possible . . . but there were rumors last year that Japanese researchers were coming close. Language is already possible. . . . You may have read about the translation software that came out in July. You speak to the computer in French, for instance, and it repeats what you said in English. *Star Trek* stuff, huh? Amazing stuff. Okay. It's been nice to see you again. I missed you people over the summer. See you tomorrow.''

Then Mrs. Webster came in. She was fun to listen to, and she made ancient Egypt sound as real as if she had lived there herself.

After school I walked into the hallway feeling dazed. I had never had a school day go by so fast in my entire life. My brain was jumping. From what Mr. Danners had taught us in one day I could already understand the basics of what it would take to program a computer to understand language. There would be a lot of things to figure out as you went but . . .

''Do your parents pick you up?''

It was Grady, walking along beside me. She was tall. I glanced down. She was actually wearing cowboy boots. I shook my head. ''No. I live pretty close. I walk.''

''My mother has to drive me in and out every day,'' she said. ''It takes almost an hour to get to the ranch.''

''Ranch?'' I said, as we turned the corner and started down the stairs. Grady said it sort of like ''ri-unch.''

Grady laughed. ''Kind of. We call it that. No cattle, though. My parents raise and train Arabian horses.''

We went through the big double doors and I saw Eddie, waiting on the sidewalk. I said good-bye to

44

Grady and watched as she climbed into a pickup truck beside a woman who was wearing a cowboy hat. For a second I thought there was someone else in the truck, but it was a big dog. A Great Dane, maybe. He licked at Grady's face as she opened the door and she had to push him back to make enough room to get in. There was loose hay in the back of the truck and it swirled as they drove off. Grady leaned out the window and waved at me.

I went toward Eddie, feeling good. He didn't say a word as we walked through the park and crossed the street. For once, I didn't get mad at him for seeming to be a thousand miles away. In fact, maybe I was beginning to understand. He was probably full of his own thoughts. I sure was. Things that Mr. Danners had said kept running through my mind.

When I got home, my mom was already there. She'd taken off early from the lab to hear about my first day. I was excited and she kept smiling and saying that she'd just known I would like Tillison. Parents love to tell you that they already knew something that you just found out for yourself. Sometimes it makes me mad, but I was feeling too good to let anything bother me very much.

All that afternoon, I talked to my mother about regular, sensible things, and right after dinner my dad called. I told him about school and he told me about the dig. He said that they had found a really interesting temple, one that was in better shape than a lot of the other ones they had found, so they were hoping that more things would be preserved inside it. He said there were big lizards there, iguanas, that the Mayan Indians caught and ate. I made a yuck noise and he laughed and said they tasted like roast chicken. After I said

45

good-bye to him, he talked to my mom for a long time. I went toward my room, feeling good.

I had spent almost a whole day without thinking about *The Mad Inventor's Handbook*. I was pretty sure that I was a normal kid again. But then the doorbell rang, and there wasn't anybody there.

CHAPTER FIVE

My mother answered it. She made a startled, gasping sound and I ran to see what was the matter. "No one is here," she said in a puzzled voice. She was stooping down to pick something up. When she turned around, *I* made a gasping sound.

"What is this?" she asked, fiddling with the bright green string that held the bundle together. "Some kind of sheepskin?"

I reached out to take it from her, then I remembered the tingle and snatched my hands back. That tingle scared me. I hadn't wanted to feel it again. Ever. Or maybe I did want to. I didn't know. My mother was looking at me.

"Mathilda? What is this? Do you know?" She undid the string and the skin rolled out, cream colored and very curly. A note on jade green paper fluttered to the floor. I picked it up.

Mrs. Hannover had perfect, old-fashioned handwriting. *Thought you might need this soon,* the note said. She hadn't even signed it. I looked up at my mother. "It's a . . . ah . . . a present from Mrs. Hannover."

My mother nodded slowly. "The woman who rides the bike a lot? She seems very nice."

I nodded. "She is." I was staring at the cream-colored, curly sheepskin in my mother's hand. "Does it make your hands feel . . . funny?" I blurted out. My mother looked at me like I had asked if elephants laid eggs.

"My hands? No. Matt, you've been acting very strangely lately. I thought you were just nervous about school and that it would pass. But if there's something we need to talk about . . . ?"

"Of course not," I mumbled, trying to smile. All at once I reached out and took the sheepskin out of my mother's hands. My palms started tingling instantly. All I knew was that I wanted that sheepskin, and that I needed some time alone, to think. Or try to think, anyway. "It'll look nice in my bedroom," I said, way too loudly. My mother was still staring at me when I turned and ran down the hall into my room.

I spread the skin out on my bed very quickly then stepped back. The minute I took my hands away, they stopped tingling. I glanced up at *The Mad Inventor's Handbook* on the bookshelf and then back at the skin. Before I could do anything else, Mom knocked on my door.

She was holding a thick white envelope in her hands. "I was going to save this for a surprise later on," she said, smiling. "But maybe now is a good time to give it to you. I've been looking for cloth that would work, but maybe . . ." She pointed at the sheepskin on my bed and handed me the envelope.

It was a sewing pattern. A pattern for making a life-size stuffed toy dog. The picture on the front looked almost exactly like the picture on that old kid's book

48

that I keep . . . the picture of the dog that I named Jaspar when I was five. If the pattern came out as real looking as the picture, you would almost think that it was a real dog. I held the pattern so tightly that my fingernails looked white. I was nervous for a very good reason. As soon as I had touched the pattern my hands had started tingling again.

"Matt? Your dad has to go to New York this week-end," my mother was saying. I glanced up, then looked back down at the pattern. The picture on the front looked so real. Mom was still talking but I really couldn't concentrate on what she was saying.

"Matt, are you listening?" she asked. I looked up from the pattern and forced myself to watch her lips moving so that I could understand her.

"I called Nancy Meyer. She said you could stay with them if you wanted. Or, you can go with me to meet your dad in New York. It's up to you. I'm going to spend most of my time with Aunt Frances, though. She's been sick. And your father will have meetings. But if you want . . . Matt, is something wrong?"

I swallowed. "Huh?"

"Your dad has to fly to New York for a few days of meetings and then he'll go back to Mexico again," she said in a patient voice. "I can manage a couple days off from work, so I'm going to go meet him. While I'm in New York, I can see Aunt Frances. Are you all right?"

I nodded. "Sure. Of course I am." I laid the pattern down and my fingers quit tingling. I looked at her. "Thanks for the pattern, Mom. I don't know if I want to cut it up . . . the . . . the sheepskin," I added, trying to sound at least semi-normal. "Thank you. Thanks a lot."

She laughed and ruffled my hair. I didn't have the strength to object. "I'm glad you like the pattern," she said, smiling. "I thought it looked exactly like the picture on that old book. Remember what you named him?"

"Jaspar," I whispered. I felt myself making a decision. It was like something that had been sloshing around inside my brain had slowly become solid and real. Mrs. Hannover had sent me the sheepskin and said all those things . . . like she had known all along what I had been thinking about doing. Now my mother had given me the pattern and she was talking about leaving for a few days. I felt like the whole world was arranging itself so that I could try. Well, all right then. I could take a hint. Okay, okay, *okay*. Crazy or not, I was going to do it. My mother was still talking.

"I know it isn't the same as a real dog, and I'm not much of a seamstress, but I think we can do it. Matt, about going to New York . . . you'd miss a day of school if you went, which might not be a good idea this early in the year. But I know you want to see Dad, too. It's up to you."

"Here," I croaked. "I want to stay here." I couldn't quite think straight. But I knew I wasn't going anywhere. My mom and dad would both be gone. I could find some way to get rid of Eddie. It was perfect. Next weekend. Next weekend I would try it. *The Mad Inventor's Handbook* was such an *old* book. I was going to have to make a lot of adjustments and modifications. I had a lot of questions to ask Mr. Danners, and . . . I realized abruptly that my mother was still staring at me.

"Sure," I said, smiling. I sounded very sensible. Which was amazing. "I'll stay with Eddie and his mom. It'll be fun, and I really shouldn't miss school now.''

My mother looked at me closely, then nodded and went to start dinner. I sat on my bed and opened the pattern. I laid the pieces out over the sheepskin. It was the perfect size. Then I ran to my desk to check my calendar. There would be a full moon this weekend. *The Mad Inventor's Handbook* had said that there had to be a full moon, and there would be. I took a deep breath. It was a little scary how perfect everything was.

The next day at school I paid attention so hard that I got a headache. I got a chance to ask a couple of my questions. Mr. Danners looked at me and grinned. ''You pick this stuff up fast, don't you? We'll have fun this year, Matt.''

I grinned back, thinking that if he knew why I was asking the questions he would probably help my mother pick out a good counselor for me. If this incredible project worked—it would be partly because he was such a good teacher. Mrs. Webster was a great teacher too. But while she was talking about mummies, my mind was wandering.

After school I walked down the stairs with Grady and Shernoz. Shernoz really was nice. I liked her. I liked Grady, too. She was always so funny. ''I have the Tillison headache,'' she said as she went down the stairs. She pronounced it, ''hey-ad-ay-ek.'' Shernoz smiled and nodded, looking shyly at me.

''We call it that,'' she explained. ''When they give you so much in one day that it seems your mind cannot hold it all.''

I nodded. I really did have a headache. I couldn't

wait to get home. My mom wouldn't be there until five-thirty because she was behind on some work at the lab. I had my key and strict orders to call Eddie's mother the minute I got there.

I waved good-bye to Grady and Shernoz when I saw Eddie waiting on the sidewalk. We crossed the park without talking. I was too busy thinking to talk. When I got off the elevator, I was so eager to get home and look at *The Mad Inventor's Handbook* that I ran down the hall.

"Mathilda, I've told you that running in the halls is against the rules," a loud, grumpy voice called out behind me. It was Mr. Norris, of course. Who else could sound so mean? I skidded to a clumsy stop, dropping most of my books. Papers floated around, then settled on the floor. I tried hard not to scream.

"I've told you before, Mathilda," Mr. Norris said as he came down the hall toward me. "Do I need to speak to your parents?" I bit my lip, kept my mouth shut, and picked up my books. The last thing I needed right then was Mr. Norris and his stupid rules.

"It's rude not to answer when someone speaks to you, Mathilda," he said.

I looked up at him. "I forgot the rule," I said slowly. "I'll try to remember."

He was scowling. "Trying isn't enough. It isn't fair to the other people here to have kids running up and down the halls."

I just wanted to get away from him. I could feel the courage draining out of me as I stood there. It was hard to believe in magic when I was looking at Mr. Norris. I couldn't keep my mouth shut no matter how hard I tried. "I said I was sorry, okay?" I said, too loudly.

52

His frown deepened. "That's the trouble with you kids today. You don't have any respect for others."

"I do too respect other people," I almost shouted. His face went stiff and his gray hair almost bristled.

"That's about enough, Mathilda," he said coldly. "I have a very nice building here and I intended to keep it that way. You either follow the rules, or I'll speak to your mother. Do I need to do that this time?"

"No," I said finally, looking back down at the carpet. Mr. Norris just stood there with his hands on his hips while I got the last of my books off the floor. Then I walked-walked-WALKED down the hall. Once I was in our apartment, I ran to my room and threw my books on my bed. I threw them *hard*.

Mr. Norris would be pretty upset if this incredible project I was planning really worked. He sure would. I imagined him trying to make us move, then finding out that he couldn't. He'd be furious and there wouldn't be anything he could do about it. I felt myself calming down. Good. I was going to need to be calm so that I could concentrate.

CHAPTER SIX

I pulled down *The Mad Inventor's Handbook* and turned to the last section. My hands started tingling immediately, but I ignored them. I had to get organized. It said that in order to make the magic work you had to have an "Actual, organic calciferous skeleton." And three strands of "genuine hair." It also said that "the skin must be natural as well, shaped as intended and in good condition." I kept reading. It got stranger and stranger. There was the part that said you had to have a full moon—and it said that you had to have "a portion of natural spittle and nails to be included with the mixture as the incantations are read by moonlight." I set the book down and got some notebook paper. I started making a list, checking off what I already had.

It didn't say anywhere that the skin had to be a dog's skin . . . but it was hard to be sure. I sure couldn't figure out where I would get a dog's skin. It was too yucky to think about. So the sheepskin would just have to work. Since a coyote was a lot like a dog, the skeleton should work fine. The hair was in my drawer . . . from the day when Mr. Norris almost scared the dog into the street. What else? I checked my calendar again to make sure. By Friday the moon would be full. Perfect. That left only and nails and spittle and the magic part was taken care of.

I almost laughed. How was I going to get dog spit? Sometimes dogs drool, you know? But . . . I couldn't picture myself running around after somebody's dog with a glass tube trying to collect a sample. And nails? Where would I get dog's toenails? Yuck. Double yuck. But it was either that or give up, and I wasn't about to give up now. I would have to figure out a way.

I started a second list. I wasn't exactly making a simple monster like the book described. The computer components could come right out of my mother's closets. I had one set of expansion boards that I had started to put into a computer once, but then my Christmas present had been a new computer with more ROM than I needed anyway. The boards would sure come in handy now. So would some of the other junk from my mother's closets. I checked the list over and over until I was pretty sure that I could get everything I needed. This stuff was easier, even though it would take a lot of work to figure it all out. It was the ''spittle and nails'' that had me worried.

When I heard my mother's key in the lock I remembered that I had forgotten to call Mrs. Meyer to tell her I was home. I apologized before my mother had a chance to say anything, and promised that I wouldn't forget again. I meant it. I was going to have to stay completely out of trouble. I made myself do my math homework. I didn't want to get behind. I liked Mr. Danners, and I wanted him to like me. He might not ever know it, but he was going to be giving me a lot of help with my . . . project.

Right before bedtime, I went into the bathroom and found an empty aspirin container. I washed it out and put it in a zippered compartment in my notebook. I found a pair of nail clippers, too, the kind that fold up and fit in your pocket. I figured I might as well be ready, in case a chance came up. Then I went to bed.

The next morning, I started watching for dogs in the park while Eddie and I walked to school. There were a few, on leashes or running along behind a jogger. My parents had a few friends who had dogs, too, but it would look pretty funny to suddenly ask to go see people that I really didn't care that much about. My mom would want to know why and I sure couldn't see myself explaining that I needed "spittle and nails." A few times, I thought about just asking someone in the park if I could clip his dog's nails. I couldn't do it. Imagine explaining to someone you didn't know that you needed dog's nails and a little bottle filled with dog "spittle." Riiiight. So by the time I got to school on Wednesday morning, I was getting pretty worried.

Eddie and I said good-bye on the steps. Or as close as Eddie ever came to saying good-bye. What he said was, "You're acting weirder and weirder, you know that?" And he walked away.

I started to get upset, but then I didn't. I had been ignoring him a lot lately. I promised myself that I would at least try to talk to him on the way home.

Mr. Danners was pacing before we even got our computers booted up. When he started talking, I switched my mind into high gear. You had to, just to keep up with what he was saying. Toward the end of the day, he explained our homework for the rest of the month. He wanted us to create programs that incorporated the stuff that we were talking about in class.

We could do anything we wanted. We could develop a program that helped people decide when to wash the kitchen floor, he said, but it had to include the kind of language-response programming we had been learning about. We didn't have computers that were equipped to respond to a human voice, but he was going to get one that we could take turns with. Then he started explaining the details. Everything was happening too perfectly. All during social studies, I had to force myself to listen. Leaving school, I was so excited that Grady had to yell to get my attention.

"Matt!" she bellowed. I loved the way she said my name. It came out sort of like "May-yut." I turned around. Shernoz was walking with her. I stopped and waited for them.

Shernoz was smiling a dreamy smile. "They gave me the headache today, for certain," she said in her soft voice.

Grady hooted—she made a loud yahoo kind of a sound sometimes, even in class—and her voice echoed off the high white ceilings and the polished floors. Three or four kids turned to look. Grady just grinned and hooked her thumbs through her belt loops and everyone turned back around. They were used to her.

"I am beyond the Tillison headache, girls," she said. "I am flat having trouble keeping up. I mean it. Danners is all right for your computer genius types, but not for me."

Shernoz laughed quietly. "Grady is possibly the best among us, Matt. Don't let her persuade you to feel sorry for her."

Grady made a face and swept her hands out from her sides. She whopped a boy in the back and apologized to him, then she spread her hands wide again.

57

"Does this look like one who is 'the best among us'? No. This looks like someone who has been completely confused by practically everything for the last two days."

Shernoz smiled gently. The filmy cloth of her dress flared out as we went down the stairs. She put a finger to her lips and smiled. "Well, Grady," she said, "not me. Perhaps Matt will volunteer."

I looked at them. "For what?"

Grady smiled broadly. "To help me, ma'am, so I don't flunk."

I shook my head. "Grady, I'm struggling with this stuff, too. I could talk to you about it, but I'm no expert."

She jumped down the last two stairs and whirled to face us. "Thank you, ma'am. I just need somebody to go over it with sometimes. We can do it on the phone if your parents don't mind. It's not long distance or anything. . . . I don't live that far out of town. And, believe me, I would be real grateful."

I braced my notebook against a wall and wrote down my phone number for her. Grady took it with a flourish, snatching it from my hand and spinning around with her arms out. A girl who was walking past swerved and nearly dropped her books. I looked at Grady. She never got embarrassed, no matter what she did. And almost everybody liked her. I sure did. I spotted Eddie on the sidewalk, standing by himself.

All the way home, I was on the lookout for dogs, but I remembered to try to talk to him. "How's your class going?"

He frowned and walked a little faster. "It's okay, I guess. Interesting and everything. But something else is weird."

I looked at him. "Weird?"

He looked at me straight on, instead of talking to the space above my head as usual. "Mrs. Hannover keeps telling me that I'm supposed to help you with something. She won't explain it and I don't know what she's talking about."

"Neither do I," I told him, trying to look casual. I had no intention of telling anyone what I was thinking about trying. Mrs. Hannover seemed to know already, and that made me as nervous as anything else about this whole magic business.

Eddie cleared his throat. "She's usually . . . she's usually right, somehow, even when she's weird." He looked at me sidelong, watching my face. "You know what I mean?"

"I know," I said. "But listen, Eddie, you don't have to help me with anything. She just wants us to be friends, I think."

Eddie nodded, but then he shook his head. "Maybe. She sounds so serious, like it's life and death or something. She says stuff like she's reading my mind lately. It's weird."

I know, I thought. I know, I know, I *know*. I tried to think of something else to say, but Eddie was looking away again, his eyes distant and unfocused like always. I walked along in silence, grateful that he had stopped talking. Maybe he would just forget it. I could hope so, anyway. If I tried to explain what I was doing he would think I was the weird to end all weirds. We got home without his saying anything more, and I was glad. Very glad.

Grady called me that night. She talked loudly, even over the phone. We went through our notes and she asked me questions I couldn't answer, but they made

59

me think. Usually we worked the problem out between us. We wrote down questions we wanted to ask Mr. Danners. I liked talking to her.

"I did this last year with Shernoz," she said after we had finished. "But she said it made things worse for her . . . even more confusing. She likes to think things through on her own. Your friend Eddie is like that, you know. I've had study groups with him and he never says a word, just stares at the ceiling."

I smiled. "I know."

"And when he does talk he sounds like a jerk half the time," Grady said slowly. "But I think he's just lonely and doesn't know how to be nice."

I had never thought about it like that but it made sense. "Maybe," I said slowly. "But he's not really my friend, Grady."

"That's too bad," she told me. " 'Cause that boy could sure use one. Well, I'll see you tomorrow . . . and thanks. I think I'm beginning to understand this stuff."

"Anytime you want, we can go over notes," I said, and I meant it. I liked Grady. Just then, I heard a terrible racket from her end of the line.

"That's our dogs," she practically shouted, so that I could hear her. "They bark like that whenever the hay truck goes by."

"How many do you have?" I shouted back. "I like dogs a lot." That was true of course, but I was also getting the glimmer of an idea.

"Four," Grady said, a little more quietly. The dogs were barking less. "Two Great Danes and two dachshunds. They look pretty funny when they play." I pictured that for a minute and almost started laughing. Then I bit my lip. I didn't quite know how to invite myself to meet someone's dog, but if I was going to be ready before my mother left, I had to. So I did.

"Grady, do you think I could play with one of your dogs a little one day after school? I mean, I've noticed that your mom usually brings one . . . and I'd just like to pet him and stuff. . . . I really wish I could have a dog and . . ." I trailed off, feeling myself blush. I didn't know Grady very well, really. What if she made fun of me? But she didn't.

"Sure," she said. Actually, she said "shoo-ooer." "Mom brings Rico in almost every day because he loves to ride in the truck. Maybe we can take him over into the park or something and you can play with him."

"I'd really like that," I said, trying not to sound as excited and shaky as I felt. We got off the phone. My mother was at her desk in her room. When she's working she never notices me unless I make a lot of noise. So I didn't. I raided a few closets, tiptoeing up and down the hall. I stacked the stuff in my closet, underneath dirty clothes and coats and my sneakers. I was ready, almost.

CHAPTER SEVEN

I went to school on Thursday feeling so excited that I thought I might not make it through the day. Somehow I was going to have to find a way to get a little of Rico's saliva into the old aspirin container and clip at least two of his toenails. I sure couldn't explain to Grady that I wanted a little "spittle" and a "portion of nails" from her dog. I would have to think of a way to distract her.

The day went by v-e-r-y slowly. In the morning, Mr. Danners worked with Shernoz and Devin Yen a lot. The rest of us listened or went ahead with our own projects. Everyone but me, anyway. I couldn't think about anything except the "project" I had to keep secret. In the afternoon Gayle Webster's English and social studies classes were really interesting, but I had trouble paying attention.

Two or three times Grady leaned over and whispered to me. At least she thought she was whispering. Grady whispers louder than most people talk. You could hear it clear across the room.

"Matt, are you all right today?" she kept asking.

I kept nodding and smiling. But I wasn't all right. I

had been up late too many nights in a row, getting ready. Now, *everything* depended on getting the last two things I needed. When the final bell rang, I leaped to my feet, nearly knocking my desk over.

As we came down the steps, Grady's mother was standing beside the truck holding Rico on a leash. Grady introduced me to her mom. I tried to be polite, but all I could do was stare at Rico. He was absolutely huge. He looked like a pony, not a dog. Grady's mother said that she had a few errands to run and that she'd come back in half an hour. I thanked her, trying to calm down. Grady took Rico's leash.

Rico walked along peacefully enough, his toenails clicking on the pavement, as we crossed the street. Then he saw the park in front of us and started straining against the leash. It was all Grady could do to hang on to him. Once we were in the park, she unclipped the leash from his collar and he ran.

"Rico is used to having lots of room," Grady explained, grinning. "He loves to run." He sure did. I watched him bounding around, running away from us then coming back, streaking past us then turning again. Finally Grady called him and he came toward us, loping, then trotting, then slowing to a striding walk. I set my notebook down and pretended to check my papers for a second. When I stood up, the little plastic aspirin bottle and the clippers were in my pocket. I was ready. But how could I get Grady to look away for a minute?

Stupid ideas kept coming into my mind . . . like the old kid's trick when you yell, "LOOK!" and then point in the other direction. But that wouldn't give me enough time even if Grady fell for it. I felt like screaming. All the late nights and all the planning, and now I couldn't think of something as simple as a way to distract Grady. She picked up a stick and handed it to me. "Throw it for him."

I was miserable, but I had to pretend to be having fun. Rico bounded after the stick. You had to stand still when he brought it back, because if you moved he might hit you, Grady said, by accident. It would be like getting hit by a train. Rico was *big*. I threw the stick again and again. The whole time I was trying desperately to think of some way to distract Grady.

I was still trying when we heard Grady's mother calling from the curb. We walked back and I stood there, helpless, by the pickup truck. They would leave in a minute. In one lousy little minute, everything would be ruined. I kept clenching my fists and digging my fingernails into my palms. I had to think of something. I had to—and I couldn't. I probably would have burst into tears, except for Eddie. Somehow, I had forgotten all about Eddie. But he hadn't forgotten about me.

"Hey, what's the matter with you, anyway?" he yelled when he saw me. He was furious. His eyes were narrow behind his thick glasses and his face was red.

Grady and her mother glanced at each other, then at me. I shrugged. "I forgot to tell him where I was going. We usually walk home together."

Eddie came closer, ignoring Grady and her mother. "I've been trying to figure out if you got kidnapped or what. I've been all over the school and everywhere else I could think of. Mrs. Hannover keeps telling me to be nice to you, but she doesn't know how weird you are." He was so mad that he kept shaking his head . . . which was making his glasses slip down his nose.

I was amazed that he hadn't just gone home and not worried about where I was. I smiled at him. I was very, very glad to see him, even if he did look angry enough to hit me. He was my last chance. "Eddie," I whispered. I leaned toward him like I was embarrassed and was telling him to be quiet. At least I was hoping that's what Grady and her mother would think.

"Remember what Mrs. Hannover said about helping me?" I whispered. He frowned, but he didn't move away. "Eddie, I need your help right now. Please. Just distract Grady and her mother." I breathed the words. "I need three minutes alone with this dog."

Eddie glanced at Rico. "You're weird," he whispered back. "You're the weirdest person I've ever known."

I glanced up at Grady and her mother. They were being polite and talking quietly to each other without looking at us.

"Okay, so I'm weird," I hissed. "And you have every right to be mad. But Eddie . . . you just have to help me."

Eddie shook his head. "I don't have to do anything."

"Eddie, please," I pleaded. I'm sure I looked like I was about to cry, because I *was* about to cry. Grady and her mother were still talking. They had moved a little way away from us. "Eddie. Please. PLEASE. Just get them talking or something, so I can have a minute with the dog." Rico was sitting beside me, looking around and panting.

Eddie squinted. "I know you don't have a boyfriend to be alone with but this is pretty—"

"Weird." I finished for him, forcing myself to whisper. "Eddie . . . it *is* weird. And I can't explain it."

He pushed his glasses up higher on his nose. "You've been acting weird for weeks. All this weird

65

stuff about helping you that Mrs. Hannover keeps telling me and—"

"I can't explain," I nearly shouted. Grady and her mother glanced up at me, then looked away and started talking again. I clenched my teeth and made myself whisper again. "I can't explain now. Just help me, Eddie, please. Please?" I was begging.

"You have to tell me everything," Eddie hissed at me. "You have to tell me what was in that box that day at Mrs. Hannover's and you have to tell me why you've been acting so weird."

"I can't," I groaned.

"You have to," Eddie told me. "Or I won't help you."

I swallowed hard. "All right," I whispered. "It's a project. Computers, sort of. I'll explain if it works." I was so desperate I was almost jumping up and down. Any seconds now, Grady's mom was going to say it was time to go.

"All right," he said, shaking his head. "All right." I felt like hugging him.

"Just go talk to Grady and her mom for a few minutes," I whispered frantically. "Get them to go around the truck where they can't see me." Eddie made a face. But he nodded. I grabbed his arm and pulled him toward Grady and her mom. I introduced him, talking so fast that my voice sounded like a cartoon character's.

"How's Danners's class this year?" Eddie asked Grady.

"Fine," she said, looking at him like he had just turned blue and orange. Grady knew that Eddie almost never talked. I crossed my fingers as Eddie said something about the school building, and walked around

66

the pickup, pointing across the street. They followed him. I whirled to run back to Rico, patting and talking to him while I frantically pulled the little plastic aspirin bottle from my pocket.

Rico had been running hard and he was panting. In about two seconds I had more ''spittle'' than I would ever need. I jammed the top on the plastic bottle and had the nail clippers out of my pocket in one second flat. As I bent over, Grady called out.

''Where's Rico?''

I stood up fast. ''He's right here with me,'' I said quickly, leaning over the hood of the truck, smiling sweetly. ''I'm just petting him. He's ah . . . he's right here.''

Grady nodded and turned back to hear something her mother was saying. I started to breathe again. Whatever it was that Eddie had them looking at was working perfectly. Their backs were toward me and the pickup blocked their view. I bent over again.

Rico's feet were enormous. I reached down and picked one up, like I was shaking hands with him. Rico nuzzled at my neck and pulled his paw away from me. I tried again, and he pulled it away and tried to lick my face. Finally, I bent my leg and set his paw on my knee. I patted him with one hand and managed to fit the little clippers over the tip of one of his claws. I squeezed . . . and a tiny black clipping fell into my hand. I managed to make three more tiny clips before Rico's paw slid off my knee. I put them in my pocket and reached down again. But Grady's voice brought me up straight.

''Are you trying to teach him to shake hands?''

I nodded, grinning ridiculously. I held the nail clippers tight in one fist so she couldn't see them. My hands were tingling, which made me even more nervous.

Grady smiled. "Ol' Rico already knows how," she said, coming around the front of the pickup. "Don't you, boy?" She put out her hand and Rico lifted his paw. They "shook" and Rico wagged his tail. Then Grady's mother was beside us, telling Grady that it was time to go. I thanked them for letting me play with Rico and I patted him good-bye. He really was a pretty dog, and he was nice, too. I waved when they drove away, and watched until the pickup was out of sight. Then I sat down on the sidewalk. My knees were shaky and my hands were tingling so much that it sort of hurt. I had everything I needed. I was ready.

"Boy, are you weird," Eddie said. I could only nod weakly. I agreed with him. A woman walked past and stared at me. I struggled to my feet and started toward home. Right foot, left foot. It was hard.

"When are you going to explain all this stuff?" Eddie demanded from behind me. I turned to face him. He stopped abruptly, his glasses sliding a little way down his nose.

"After I do it, if it works," I told him. "After the weekend." His face clouded. "Eddie, it's just too hard to explain," I said quickly. "But I will, if it works. I promise."

Eddie scowled, but I turned away from him and started walking again. He walked along behind me and he left me alone. Maybe he was too angry to say anything else. All I knew was that I was ready, and that I was going to try. If it worked, I would keep my promise. And it just might work. For the first time, I was beginning to believe it, deep down inside myself. It just might work.

When we got home I saw Mr. Norris in the lobby. He looked as grumpy as usual. I remembered to walk so that he couldn't say anything to me about running. Since my mom was going to be a little late, I called Eddie's mother to let her know I was home. After I hung up, I went into my bedroom and put the little aspirin bottle and Rico's nail clippings in my drawer. Then I pulled down *The Mad Inventor's Handbook.*

When my mother got home, I put everything away. Once she was asleep, I took it all out again and worked quietly until long after midnight. I modified the magic chants in *The Mad Inventor's Handbook* once more. Then I worked on the chants I was making up. I wrote out a final draft using a felt-tip pen with black ink. I was going to have to read them by moonlight, and I wanted to be able to see them well enough so that I didn't goof. It was hard to write neatly because my fingers were tingling. Then I turned on my computer. I started loading the microchips from my old expansion boards with data.

When I finally quit working, I had trouble falling asleep. One more day and my mother would be leaving. One more day and I would try it. I was ready. As ready as I was ever going to be.

CHAPTER EIGHT

Friday went by fast. I saw Mrs. Hannover in the lobby on my way to school. She winked at me and smiled, but didn't stop to talk. I was glad. I felt strange enough without having to wonder whether or not she could read my mind. Eddie didn't talk at all as we walked across the park. I could tell that he was upset with me. I couldn't blame him, really. But I wouldn't break my promise. I was just waiting to see if there was anything to explain or not. When we got to school he stopped on the steps.

"Too bad you're staying with us this weekend," he said without blinking. "It should be just tons of fun to have a weirdo around." Then he walked away from me. It hurt my feelings, but it didn't last. I was too excited, and too scared, and too . . . well, too *preoccupied* to care very much whether or not Eddie Meyer thought I was weird.

I managed to ask Mr. Danners a few more questions, and I borrowed one of his books to help me with the programming on my "homework project." It *would* help me with my homework, but it would help even more with the project no one could know about yet. Grady looked at me closely a few times. I think she could tell I was tired, and she was wondering what was going on. I thought about the little aspirin container and the tiny crescent-shaped clippings of Rico's toenails that were waiting for me at home. If it hadn't been for Grady, I would never have been ready in time. I felt like thanking her and Rico. Maybe I would—on Monday.

When the final bell rang I was the first one out the door. I walked so fast that Eddie could barely keep up on the way home. He still wasn't speaking to me, and as terrible as it sounds, I didn't really notice that much. I was going over and over the lists I had made in my mind, trying to make sure I had thought of everything. The chants were going to be tricky. Especially the ones I had written myself.

When I got home, my mother was waiting for me. She had stayed home from work to get ready for the trip. I tried to look and act like everything was normal. It wasn't easy. Things were about as normal as snow in July.

"Matt," my mother was saying, "I'm going to be leaving soon. Why don't you shower now and get ready to go down to Eddie's?" She ruffled my hair and I let her.

In my room I touched the sheepskin just to feel my fingers tingle. I packed my overnight bag. Then I got into the shower. I could think in there as well as anywhere else and that's what I needed to do now. I knew that I wasn't going to Eddie's. I knew that I had to think of something. And I did.

It wasn't that hard, really. My mother wanted to walk me down to Eddie's, but I made up an excuse about wanting to take a book to show him that I couldn't find. I told her I had to look for it, but I would go down as soon as I found it. She told me to hurry, that Mrs. Meyer was expecting me, and reminded me to take my key. Then we hugged and she was gone.

I called Eddie's mother and told her I wasn't feeling very well, and that I wanted to lie down for a while. I *wasn't* feeling all that good really, so I guess I sounded convincing enough. She told me to call them if I needed anything, and reminded me to lock the door. Then she said she would call later to see how I was doing. I thanked her and hung up. For a second I just stood there, staring at the wall. Then I got to work.

The Mad Inventor's Handbook had very clear directions, but I didn't want to follow them exactly. I wasn't making a monster that would stomp around all clumsy and scary and stupid. With everything that I had learned from Mr. Danners, I was going to make sure that Jaspar was really smart—that he would be able to understand everything I said. I got everything out of the closet and just sat there for a while, going over my notes. Then I began to put things together.

My hands tingled so much that I was clumsy at first. I still didn't know exactly what the tingling meant, or why it happened, but I got used to it as I worked.

I had to rewire the skeleton three times before I got it exactly right. Twice, I almost quit. It was silly . . . maybe even sort of crazy. I knew that. But *The Mad Inventor's Handbook* said that if you really believed in the magic, and if you wanted with all your heart and mind and will for it to work—it would. Besides, I had a lot more going for me than the magic. I was using the latest computer technology, and I had figured out a way to cover all my modifications by adding to *The*

Mad Inventor's Handbook's magic chants. At least I *thought* I had.

I used Mr. Danners's book to finish loading the microchips with language-response data. I fit them along the spine of the coyote skeleton, then worked the rest of the electronic components into place. I double and triple checked everything. Then I checked it all again. Part of the time I was calm, and part of the time I was trembling.

I arranged the stuffed toy pattern pieces on the sheepskin. I cut them out, then followed the directions and sewed the pieces together very, very carefully. When I fit the sheepskin cover onto the skeleton, it wasn't quite right. I made a few adjustments and tried again. The second time, it was perfect. I made one last check to see that all the electronic components were in place—then I used the stuffing from an old pillow to fill out the shape. I took a deep breath. That was it. I sewed the sheepskin closed.

When I was finished I stood back, breathing hard, like I had been running. He really looked like Jaspar. The sheepskin had been hard to cut and even harder to sew, but it fit perfectly over the skeleton now. The long curly hair covered the seams, and the fake eyes and eyelashes that had come with the pattern looked real. Almost too real. I shivered.

For a few minutes I just sat there, telling myself that I had gone just a little cuckoo, but no one ever had to find out about it if I stopped right now. I could just tell my mother I'd made the toy dog while she was gone. I almost decided to quit. I was scared, I guess.

But somehow I just couldn't give up. I had wanted a dog as long as I could remember, but every apartment we had ever lived in had a rule against dogs.

73

Jaspar would look like a dog, sure. But no one could ever say he was against the rules. Not even mean old Mr. Norris. I pictured Mr. Norris's face. If everything worked the way *The Mad Inventor's Handbook* said it would, Mr. Norris was going to be about as surprised as a person can be. I couldn't wait to tell him that Jaspar wasn't really a dog. But Mr. Norris wasn't the reason I was doing this. I wanted Jaspar more than I had ever wanted anything in my life. That was reason enough to try—no matter how crazy it seemed.

I reached for *The Mad Inventor's Handbook* and gathered up my notes. It was getting dark out, but I didn't want to turn on the lights. If I did I'd have to wait for my eyes to get used to the dark when I turned them off again. I had to read the magic chants by moonlight. I looked out my window, toward the park. The moon was rising.

I found a glass bowl in the kitchen to make the magic potion in. The instructions said you couldn't use metal or "crockery"—it had to be "clear and transparent glass." I mixed things exactly the way the instructions said to do it. I started with plain, clear water, and a pinch of salt. I had no idea what the salt was for, but it said to use it, so I did. Then I added the "second portion of clear water."

Then, holding the bowl carefully, I looked out my bedroom window. I just stood there, watching the sky until it was dark out and the moon was up a little higher. Perfect. I opened the curtains wide, so that the moonlight came in and fell on the bowl. The glass felt cool and smooth in my hands. I got back to work.

The "spittle and nails" went in next, one at a time. Then one of the "genuine hairs" from the black dog that had run across the street. After each thing there was a little chant to say . . . or a little motion to make with my hand. Sometimes both. Then I read the chants that I had written out, about Jaspar being able to understand me when I talked and stuff.

My hands were tingling but I could feel that the coolness of the bowl was changing. It was starting to feel warm, as if the moonlight were really hot sunlight and the water was heating up. I read the magic chants slowly. Every word had to be perfect. I was concentrating so hard that the ceiling could have fallen in and I wouldn't have noticed.

When the potion was finished, I set the bowl in front of Jaspar and walked around him three times, repeating more of the magic words, like the instructions said to do. It felt strange, like I was walking on clouds instead of carpet. Then I sat in front of Jaspar, facing the window, in the patch of moonlight.

I held two black hairs from the real dog between the third and fourth fingers of my right hand . . . exactly like it said to do. I rested my left hand on Jaspar's curly head, took a deep breath, and said the next part of the chants. Then I picked up the bowl in both hands and dribbled some of the liquid on Jaspar's face like it said to do in *The Mad Inventor's Handbook*. I held the bowl in my lap and tried very, very hard to believe that it would work—that it *was* working.

I closed my eyes and whispered. "I believe in magic. I do. I want this to work with all of my heart, my mind, and my will." I meant it, I meant it, I *meant* it. I wanted Jaspar so much.

Concentrating as hard as I knew how, I read the final chants out of the book very slowly, careful to pronounce every single word exactly right. As I said the final words, the water in the bowl started to bubble and steam—even though it didn't feel hot enough to be boiling. My hands and my arms were tingling all the way up to my elbows. I could *feel* the magic starting to work. I raised the bowl over my head the way the instructions told me to do, holding my breath.

"What in the world are you *doing*, Mathilda?"

Mr. Norris's voice came from right behind me. It was loud, grumpy, and startled me so badly that I started to jump up, lost my balance—and threw the glass bowl backward, straight at him. I heard him gasp as I whirled around, scrambling to my feet.

It was hard to stand up. I felt off balance. Everything was spinning inside me. Mr. Norris was dripping wet. He looked like he wanted to strangle me. I was about as confused as I could be. But I knew one thing. I had felt the magic working and now Mr. Norris had ruined everything. Everything that I had been worrying about and working toward was *gone*. Ruined, gone, completely *destroyed*. My mouth started working a couple of seconds before my voice did.

". . . dare you just come in here?" I screamed. "How dare you?"

Mr. Norris wiped at his face with his hand. "Lower your voice, young lady." He was yelling, too. "Mrs. Meyer tried to call you, but you didn't answer your phone. She asked me to check on you. I rang the bell, but you didn't bother to answer that either. I used my passkey to get in." He was practically spitting the words at me. *"You* have no right to worry people like this. And now, this—" He gestured at the bowl on the floor and my piles of notes. "You can be very sure that I'm going to talk to your parents about all this. You shouldn't be left unsupervised for a minute, Mathilda Jameson. Not for . . . fora . . . forawwrrr . . . *awwrrrrf."*

76

I stared at him. The strangest thing I had ever seen in my whole life was happening to Mr. Norris. He was shrinking and changing shape at the same time. In the dim moonlight his face seemed to scowl deeper as he got smaller. He looked blurry. I rubbed my eyes and blinked. He kept shrinking and changing, his legs and arms kept getting shorter . . . until there was a gray bulldog standing in the doorway instead of a man. The bulldog looked at me and snarled. I tried to swallow but my throat was too dry. Way too dry.

I heard a soft rustling sound behind me. I spun around.

Jaspar was standing up, stretching like dogs do when they have been asleep for a long time. I stared at him. It had worked? It had! It had worked! I dropped to my knees and hugged Jaspar. His curly fur was warm against my cheek. I felt myself starting to cry a little, the way you do when you are just too full of happy feelings to hold them all. Jaspar was real, he was here, he was finally mine. Then I remembered Mr. Norris. I turned to look at him.

He was still standing in the doorway, his bulldog face scowling. I watched him lift one front paw up and stare at it with a puzzled expression. He bent around to look over his back. His stumpy tail flopped to one side, then the other while he watched it. He looked up at me and growled. Then he turned slowly and started out the door, swaying from side to side like a small, furry sailor who has forgotten how to walk on dry land.

I wasn't sure of very much right then, but I was sure that I shouldn't let him go. I leaped to my feet—and immediately fell down. My hands had stopped tingling but now they were shaking. So were my knees. And my thoughts. Jaspar was watching me. I reached out to touch his head, trying hard to think.

Mr. Norris had been changed into a bulldog. A short, grumpy bulldog. I felt laughter and fear rising side by side in my throat. They jammed against each other and got stuck. I tried getting up again. This time I made it. I stood there, trying to organize my feet. Jaspar was looking up at me.

"Stay right here, Jaspar," I told him. He looked at me and tilted his head like a curious puppy. "I'll be back in just a minute," I promised him. He yawned and lay back down. He seemed to understand me. So everything had worked—even the part of the chants I had written! I forced my left foot to take a step and that seemed to help the right one remember what to do. I staggered down the hallway.

"Mr. Norris, come back," I called shakily. My voice was about as steady as the rest of me. The hallway was dark and it felt like it was a hundred miles long. I flipped on lights as I went. "Mr. Norris?" There was no answer. I couldn't stop staggering so I tried to stagger faster.

When I rounded the corner, Mr. Norris was crossing the living room, lifting his paws one at a time and setting them down carefully, as though walking felt strange to him. As I headed toward him, he snarled and broke into an awkward trot toward the entry hall.

"Stop, Mr. Norris," I pleaded. My thoughts were running in tight little circles, and my feet kept getting mixed up. Mr. Norris had gotten to the front door, and it was closed. He sat on the carpet and looked up at the doorknob. He couldn't reach it, and even if he could have, he couldn't open it. Bulldogs can't open doors. He growled at me over his shoulder. He looked

78

so furious and so helpless that I giggled. He growled louder.

"Maatt?"

The voice came down the hallway and I spun around so fast I almost fell down. It sounded like my cousin. He's two years old. The voice sounded scared, like a little kid in the grocery store who can't find his mother. I had to be imagining things. I looked back at Mr. Norris. He was sitting with his back to me. His stumpy tail quivered, and his ears drooped. He lifted a front paw and bent to stare at it. Then the hair along his back bristled and he growled again.

"Maatt?" the voice called once more.

I whirled and ran back into my room. Jaspar was sitting up. When I came in he blinked. He blinked and looked at me. His eyes were a deep, deep brown, with flecks of orangey color—like looking at firelight through a glass of root beer. I dropped on my knees beside him. He nuzzled my cheek, and I hugged him.

"Maatt?" he said into my ear. I tried not to start shaking again. Jaspar could talk. I wasn't sure why or how, but he could. I felt myself grinning so hard it hurt my cheeks. Then I thought about Mr. Norris and the grin wilted. I would have to change him back. Could I? And even if I could, wouldn't he be so furious with me that he would make us move whether or not Jaspar was against his rules? *What* was I going to do?

Slowly, the warmth of Jaspar's soft fur began to calm me down. Then the doorbell rang and I flinched. It had to be Mrs. Meyer. Or, if Mrs. Meyer thought I was in trouble before she called Mr. Norris and then *he* hadn't called her back or anything, she might have called the police. Could they put me in jail for changing my landlord into a bulldog? I felt a giggle forming in my throat. Then I felt like crying. The doorbell rang again.

"Whaaat is . . . what is that?" Jaspar asked, tilting his head. He sounded so sweet and so scared. I took a deep breath. Whatever else happened, I was not going to let him spend his first day with me watching me stagger around looking terrified.

"It's all right," I lied. "It's called a doorbell." My voice was a little squeaky, but Jaspar didn't seem to notice. "The doorbell means someone is here, and I have to go talk to them for a minute." I took another breath. I hugged him once more. Whether it was Mrs. Meyer or the police, I was going to have to do some fast talking. I had to think, think, THINK. "I want you to stay in here, in my room," I said, pressing my cheek into Jaspar's warm fur for a second more. "Don't be afraid and I'll be back as soon as I can. Do you understand?" I leaned back to look at him.

Jaspar nodded very solemnly. It looked so funny to see a dog nodding that I smiled and ruffled the curly hair on his head. The doorbell rang again. I forced myself to stand up. I stood there, swaying, while my feet and legs remembered what to do. I made myself go down the hallway, trying not to look like someone walking across uneven ice. "Normal," I whispered to myself. Whoever it was, I had to try to look normal. It would be hard. Very hard.

CHAPTER NINE

The doorbell was ringing. Mr. Norris was sitting in a chair in the living room, with his nose about an inch from one of his paws, staring at it. He growled at me as I went past.

"I'll be able to think of something as soon as they go away," I told him. I knew perfectly well I wasn't making sense, but I couldn't do anything about it. The doorbell rang again.

I would have to tell whoever it was that I was still feeling sick. I reached for the doorknob, knowing I probably *looked* sick enough to take to a hospital. I scrunched my face up then relaxed it and tried to look like I only needed to be left alone for a few more hours. The doorbell rang again and I realized I was just standing there, with my hand on the knob. So I opened it.

It wasn't the police. And it wasn't Mrs. Meyer either. It was Mrs. Hannover. Her blue eyes were twinkly and she was smiling. "Hello, Mathilda. Mrs. Meyer just asked me to check on you," she said cheerfully. "Mr. Norris was supposed to, but now she can't

81

reach him. She's waiting for an important phone call from her sister, or she would have come herself.''

Mr. Norris made a low growling noise in the living room, but Mrs. Hannover only raised her eyebrows a little. ''I would love to know what you did with my sheepskin, Mathilda,'' she went on. ''I haven't been able to stop sneezing for hours.''

''Sneezing,'' I echoed. Would anything ever make sense again?

Mrs. Hannover smiled. ''My nose tingles when there's magic around. I sneeze because it tickles,'' she explained in a perfectly reasonable voice.

''It's always my hands,'' I stammered, trying to think. If her nose had tingled every time my hands had, that was how she had known about the magic. It was nice to have *something* make even a little sense. I felt better. Sort of, anyway. Like when you think you forgot your spelling homework, your book report, and your math homework and then you find out that at least the book report isn't due until tomorrow.

Mrs. Hannover came in, and I closed the door behind her. ''Hands would be nicer,'' she said. ''Sneezing isn't very polite.'' Mr. Norris growled again. Mrs. Hannover looked at me questioningly. I peeked around the corner into the living room. Mr. Norris had curled up in the chair. He was growling in his sleep. Mrs. Hannover looked into the living room and her eyes widened. Then she smiled again. ''First things first. Where is your telephone?''

I lurched toward the kitchen and she followed me. I turned on the light and Mrs. Hannover picked up the phone and dialed.

''Mrs. Meyer?'' she said into the receiver. My stomach tightened. "I came up to check on Mathilda," Mrs. Hannover went on brightly. "She apologizes for any worry she caused you. She feels better now. She got so absorbed in what she was doing that she never even heard the phone ring at all. I asked her to have dinner and spend the night with me. I hope you don't mind." She winked at me. "I've been sneezing a great deal, feeling a little sorry for myself, and I would enjoy her company." She winked at me again. "No, Mr. Norris isn't here," she told Mrs. Meyer. "Perhaps he just forgot. We will call you first thing in the morning." She nodded, listening. "Of course. Thank you. Good-bye."

I let out my breath as she hung up, and I leaned back against the cool kitchen wall. Now I had until morning to figure out what to do. I could relax, a little anyway.

Mrs. Hannover was watching me. She was wearing one of her long flowing skirts with an embroidered blouse. Her silvery hair was braided and she looked like a very calm, very nice, Gypsy grandmother. She smiled and raised her eyebrows again. "Now that that's taken care of, I would love to know what is going on."

I opened my mouth to answer, then I closed it again. Mrs. Hannover nodded encouragingly. I started explaining from the beginning, because I couldn't think of any other way to do it. My voice stopped squeaking by the time I got to the part about trying to cut Rico's toenails. Mrs. Hannover laughed out loud, her hands pressed against her cheeks. I told her about the magic spells, and how I had changed them a little because I had wanted Jaspar to be smart. I told her how sweet Jaspar was, and how much I loved him already—and that somehow the magic had made it so that he could talk. She interrupted me for the first time.

83

"Jaspar will have to learn not to talk around strangers—how to act like a dog," she said. Her face was very serious. "He absolutely must have a good disguise, Mathilda."

I stood up straighter. "A disguise?"

She nodded, looking directly into my eyes. "Some people would want to study him, to see what makes him tick. Others would be frightened of him, and of you, too, because you did something they couldn't understand. It's sad, but true, Mathilda. Magic is not very welcome in the world today."

I stared at her. "But I thought that if I told everybody Jaspar was magical and not a real dog we wouldn't have to move. . . ." I stopped because she was shaking her head.

"Your parents are both scientists. They would never believe in magic, would they?"

I stared at her, feeling stupid. Mrs. Hannover was right. She was absolutely right. My mother would be the first one who would want to run scientific tests on Jaspar. There was a huge knot tightening in my stomach. I imagined Jaspar living in a cage in some laboratory. I might never see him again.

"Computer companies would want to study him once they knew that you used microchips to help make him," Mrs. Hannover went on. "Other people will say that he isn't natural. People often hate what they don't understand. You will have to protect him, Mathilda. You'll have to keep his secret."

"But if I tell everyone he's a real dog Mr. Norris will never . . ." I began. My throat had gotten so tight that I couldn't say anything more. My eyes were burning. A snoring, growling sound came from the living room.

"It will all work out," Mrs. Hannover said, smiling. "Is that Jaspar?"

The lump in my throat felt enormous. "No . . . no . . . that's Mr. Norris," I choked. If Mrs. Hannover hadn't held onto me, I might have fallen over. My brain was making noises like a car trying to start on a snowy morning. I couldn't tell anyone about Jaspar. Mr. Danners had said that the competition in the computer industry was incredible . . . they even spied on each other. Would they kidnap Jaspar? Would someone try to hurt him? Why, oh *why* hadn't I thought of any of that? And now, Mr. Norris was going to be furious with me. Worse than furious. He was going to be . . . I couldn't think of a word that could describe how mad he was going to be. And he would tell everyone. "Mr. Norris will never forgive me," I wailed.

"Calm down, and explain, Mathilda," Mrs. Hannover said gently. She propped me back against the wall. I swallowed and started talking. I expected her to be shocked, but she smiled when I described how Mr. Norris had shrunk and gotten blurry.

"Maybe he won't hate dogs so much after this," she said when I was finished. "You'll think of a way to change him back. Magic rarely comes without complications and unexpected travails. Now, then. Where is Jaspar?"

I covered my face with my hands for a minute. Everything was so mixed up. "He's in my room," I told her, talking like a little kid playing peekaboo, through my fingers.

"I want to meet him very much," Mrs. Hannover said in a reasonable voice. I nodded and led her down the hallway. She looked at Mr. Norris as we went past the living room. He was asleep, his gray fur rumpled around the deep bulldog creases in his face.

Jaspar was sound asleep in the floor by my bed. He looked so peaceful. The moonlight was bright, and I didn't want to startle him, so I didn't turn on the light. I hugged him gently and when he woke up I introduced him to Mrs. Hannover. She bent over and reached out and lifted his paw and shook it gently.

"I am very happy to make your acquaintance, Jaspar," she said softly. "I hope that we will be great friends."

Jaspar tipped his head, like dogs do when they are figuring something out. "Hello, Mrs. Hann-o-ver," he said slowly.

"You have lovely manners, Jaspar," she said, smiling.

Jaspar turned to look at me. "What are man . . . man-ners?"

I ruffled his fur. "I don't know, exactly," I admitted. "When grown-ups like the way you act, I guess. When you're being polite." He nodded, but he looked puzzled.

Mrs. Hannover straightened up. "Real manners," she said to Jaspar, "are when you think not only of yourself, but also about other people's feelings and welfare." She looked up at me. "Shall we go down to my apartment?"

I looked up at her. "Why?"

"Mrs. Meyer could call to see how we're doing, and I don't want her worrying any more tonight."

"That's manners," Jaspar said shyly.

"That's right, Jaspar!" Mrs. Hannover chirped like a first grade teacher when you get the answer right.

She was smiling and her eyes twinkled. "Jaspar is very intelligent," she whispered. I nodded and smiled back.

"Bring whatever you'll need," Mrs. Hannover said. She sat down cross-legged by Jaspar and began talking to him. I watched them for a second. Mrs. Hannover was explaining to Jaspar what we were going to do.

"What's an ele-ele-elevator?" I heard him ask.

My overnight bag was already packed, with my key in one of the zippered pockets. I took out some of the clothes and put in *The Mad Inventor's Handbook,* along with my notes and the glass bowl and everything else I could think of. I couldn't quite get the zipper closed, but it all fit. The bag had a long strap so I slung it over my shoulder and leaned down to pick Jaspar up. Mrs. Hannover stood up and smoothed her skirt. Jaspar blinked once or twice, then he put his head on my shoulder and closed his eyes.

I looked down at him and wished desperately that I could just forget about Mrs. Norris, about anyone who would hurt Jaspar. I just wanted to get to know him, take him to the park, play with him, teach him things, let Grady and my parents meet him. They would all like him. I knew they would. But it wasn't that simple. Mrs. Hannover had made me realize it never would be.

"Ready?" Mrs. Hannover asked. I nodded, feeling anything *but* ready.

Mr. Norris growled softly in his sleep when Mrs. Hannover picked him up, but he didn't wake up. He was heavier than Jaspar—and Jaspar was pretty heavy— so we walked slowly. I locked the door one-handed and Mrs. Hannover had to push the elevator button with her elbow, then we hid around the corner in case anyone was in the elevator. She peeked in. It was empty.

We got down to the lobby before Mr. Norris started to wake up. At first he was just kind of twitching, but then he really started to struggle. Mrs. Hannover had to put him down. "You can walk if you prefer it," Mrs. Hannover said to him. "But let's go quickly, Mr. Norris, please." She glanced around the lobby. "We don't want anyone to see us, before Mathilda can change you back."

Mr. Norris growled. It was an odd, long growl. He turned slowly and walked away from us, back toward the elevators. Jaspar wriggled in my arms and I saw that he was awake. "He said he doesn't like this . . . dream," he said haltingly, looking up at me. "What's a dream, Matt?"

Mr. Norris growled again, staring up at the elevator button.

"He wants to go home," Jaspar said. "He wants to go to bed so that he can wake up."

"Jaspar can understand Mr. Norris, but we can't," I said slowly. "I wonder why Mr. Norris can't talk, too."

Mrs. Hannover shrugged. "I don't know. It must have something to do with when he came in—which chants he missed. Will that help you?"

I shifted Jaspar's weight and looked at her. "Maybe. If I can figure out how to rework the chants. Let's get him down to your apartment," I added nervously. She nodded, glancing around. Mr. Norris growled again, more loudly.

"He says he's had about enough of this non-non-nonsense," Jaspar said quietly looking up at my face. "What's nonsense?"

88

"I'll tell you in a minute," I whispered into his ear. Then I raised my head.

"Mr. Norris," I began, trying to sound calm, "I know that this is all pretty hard to believe. But it isn't a dream, and going to bed won't help. We have to go down to Mrs. Hannover's now, so that I can figure out how to change you back."

He faced us, growling. His teeth showed this time.

"He's not going anywhere with you," Jaspar translated.

I felt like screaming. "Mr. Norris, please," I begged him. "We can't stay here." He just glared at me. I looked helplessly at Mrs. Hannover. "What can we do?"

"Perhaps it would help if I went down and got something we could use for a leash," she whispered. "He won't like it, but I'm afraid it might be necessary."

I nodded. It sure didn't look like Mr. Norris was going to come with us willingly, and we couldn't stand in the lobby arguing with him all night long. Mrs. Hannover hurried across the lobby and opened the door at the top of the stairs that led down to her apartment. "Try to keep him calm," she said over her shoulder as she disappeared.

"Please, Mr. Norris," I said, once she was gone. "I'm going to do everything I can to change you back." He growled again. He looked like he wanted to bite me.

Just then, the elevator doors opened. Eddie Meyer was standing there. For a second he looked startled, then he looked angry.

"Don't say anything," I whispered into Jaspar's ear. "No matter what, don't talk until I tell you it's all

89

right. Not a word. Do you understand?'' He nodded but Eddie didn't notice. I had promised to explain everything to Eddie, but now, after what Mrs. Hannover had said, I was afraid to. What if he was angry enough at me to tell people about Jaspar?

''What are you doing?'' Eddie demanded. ''Mr. Norris would have a fit if he saw these dogs in here.'' He stepped out of the elevator and the doors closed behind him. Mr. Norris growled at him. ''Hey,'' Eddie said. ''He's mean.'' He dodged around Mr. Norris, then turned and looked back at me. ''You sure upset my mom tonight,'' he said, pushing his glasses farther up on his nose. ''You're weird, you know that? My mother sent me down here to ask Mrs. Hannover to come for dinner tomorrow. Does she know about the dogs?''

I opened my mouth to say something, but since I couldn't figure out what I could possibly say, I closed it again. Eddie walked across the lobby and leaned against the big double doors, facing me. He crossed his arms.

''You're the weirdest person I've ever met,'' he said slowly, pronouncing every syllable with great care. ''Absolutely the weirdest.''

Mr. Norris walked toward Eddie, growling. Eddie stood there glaring at me and glancing nervously at Mr. Norris. ''He's really mean, Matt,'' he said uneasily. ''Does he bite?''

I opened my mouth again, but nothing would come out. Eddie was pressing against the door. Suddenly, Mr. Norris lunged forward, snarling. Eddie jumped backward and the doors swung open. Before I could do anything, Mr. Norris had shot past Eddie and was out on the sidewalk.

"He thinks it's a dream," I gasped, pushing past Eddie. Mr. Norris was running now. I chased him down the sidewalk, pleading with him to stop, to come back, but he only ran faster. Jaspar was heavy, and I couldn't run very well. Mr. Norris dashed past the taxidermy shop, then the little grocery store, then he darted around the corner. When I got there, I stopped, breathing hard. The sidewalk was empty as far as I could see. I hugged Jaspar and started crying.

CHAPTER TEN

When I heard footsteps pounding toward me, I looked up. Eddie skidded to a stop. "Mrs. Hannover came up right after you ran off, and she told me to follow you." He panted. "She said she's going to get her car and call my mom to tell her I'm spending the night, and then she'll come find us. Matt, what's going *on?*" he demanded. "All of a sudden you have two dogs and—"

"I can't explain now." I sniffled. "We have to find Mmm—the bulldog." I was shaking all over again.

Jaspar was looking up at me, his eyes wide. He was scared and I wasn't helping him at all. A car went past and he pressed against me as the headlights swept by.

I hugged him. "It's all right," I whispered into his curly fur. Then I realized I had said exactly the wrong thing, but it was too late.

"I can talk now?" Jaspar asked.

Eddie's face froze. "Who said that?" he asked in a soft, strained voice. He was staring at Jaspar.

"I said it," Jaspar told him. He twisted around to look at me. "You said that when you said it was all right that I could talk. Right?"

92

Eddie's face went absolutely, completely, white. Even his lips looked pale. He was still staring at Jaspar. I tried to smile. I probably looked like I was about to explode. Or fall down. Or scream. That's how I felt, anyway.

"That dog talked," Eddie said, without moving his lips.

I heard a high, beeping car horn and I turned toward the street. Mrs. Hannover was leaning out the window of her little sports car, waving at us.

"Let's go." I pulled at Eddie's sleeve.

"Dogs can't talk," he said in a low, uneven voice.

"Come on," I pleaded, trying to hold Jaspar and pull Eddie at the same time. His legs seemed stiff, as if his knees had locked, but I managed to drag him to the curb.

Mrs. Hannover took one look at Eddie and said, "He needs an explanation. I'll drive around a few blocks while you tell him."

I hesitated. "Explain to Eddie," Mrs. Hannover insisted. "I can cover enough area driving. You can trust Eddie. And be kind. Magic is not always easy for people to accept." Eddie was still staring at Jaspar. I frowned as Mrs. Hannover drove away.

I wasn't sure about trusting Eddie. But there wasn't much choice now.

"Magic?" Eddie said. His eyes were unfocused and his glasses had slipped down his nose.

A car went by and Jaspar flinched away from the bright headlights again. We all needed a place to calm down. I pushed Eddie's glasses up and guided him toward the little grocery store. It was closed but there were a couple of benches in front of it, and the way

93

Eddie was walking, he might fall down if he didn't sit down.

The benches were in a quiet corner behind a tree that grew next to the sidewalk. I pushed on Eddie's shoulder until he sat down, then I set Jaspar down between us. My arms were aching from holding him for so long.

"Dogs don't talk," Eddie repeated softly, staring at his knees.

"What's a dog?" Jaspar asked. When Eddie didn't answer him, he yawned and lay down, then closed his eyes. He was just like a puppy. Excitement made him sleepy. I touched the warm curly fur on his side. I would do anything to protect him. Anything.

Eddie's head jerked up and his eyebrows had arched above his glasses when Jaspar talked. Now he was drooping again. "I feel sick," he said quietly. His glasses were fogging up.

"Eddie," I said, "you have to promise that you won't ever tell anyone about Jaspar as long as you live." I waited until his eyes focused on mine before I went on. "I'll tell people you imagined it, Eddie. I'll tell them you're lying. I'll run away. I'll do something awful, if you don't promise." I knew I sounded fierce. I felt fierce. Eddie had to understand how important this was.

"That's Jaspar?" He pointed and his finger looked a little shaky. I nodded. "A dog that talks?" I waited, letting him absorb the idea. "A talking dog. Named Jaspar," he murmured.

I understood how he felt. It was still hard for me to believe everything that had happened. The problem was that we didn't have *time* for him to get all goofy. "Eddie," I said, "promise you'll never tell anyone

94

about him. People have to think he's just a regular dog. Please."

He looked at me through his misty glasses. "This has something to do with that day you acted so weird in the park with Grady and her mom, doesn't it?" I nodded. Good. His brain was starting to work again, at least a little.

I touched Jaspar lightly to make sure he was asleep. I didn't want him to hear what I was going to say. "Eddie, think about it. If people know Jaspar can talk, they'll take him away from me and make him live in a cage in a laboratory while they try to figure him out. Computer companies, movie producers, people who think he's unnatural or something—life would be awful for him. And me."

Eddie nodded, but I couldn't tell if he understood or not. I felt myself starting to panic. "Come on, Eddie," I exploded. "If you tell people about Jaspar, it'll ruin my life and his. *Please.* You have to promise. Whether we were friends before or not, I don't know. But I'm asking you to be my friend now. And Jaspar's friend."

I was practically shouting. Jaspar sat up, blinking. "What's a friend, Ed-die?"

"Answer him, Eddie," I said quietly, hoping that Eddie would see Jaspar like I did for a second. Lovable. Sweet. And in need of protection.

Eddie looked at Jaspar. His face turned pink. He looked at me, then back at Jaspar, then at me, then Jaspar again.

"Mrs. Han-nover said she was my friend," Jaspar said. "Are you my friend, Ed-die?" Jaspar asked. He wriggled around to look at me. "What's a friend?"

"Answer him," I said, looking hard into Eddie's eyes.

"A friend is somebody who cares about you, I guess," he stammered, glancing away. Then he looked back at me. "I . . . okay, Matt, okay," he said quietly, looking at Jaspar. "I promise I won't ever tell anyone about your . . . your . . . about Jaspar."

"For as long as you live," I insisted. "Swear it."

"For as long as I live, I swear I won't tell anybody about . . . Jaspar," he said. He pushed his glasses up higher on his nose. "But where did you get a . . . a talking dog?"

I knew he was going to ask something like that and I was ready.

"I made him."

I knew he would turn white again, and he did.

"You made him," Eddie echoed in a flat voice. Then he looked angry. "Matt, if he looked like a robot or something, I'd believe you. But that dog is breathing, Matt. *Breathing.*"

"I know," I said, hugging Jaspar. "I know." I took a deep breath and started talking, as fast as I could. Eddie looked sort of blank when I told him about *The Mad Inventor's Handbook.* By the time I got to "spittle and nails" he looked sick again. Then he grinned a wild grin that slowly dissolved into a frown. I knew exactly what he was feeling. All of it. He was just going through it faster than I had. When I finished he looked angry again, and his eyes were locked on mine.

"Magic?" he demanded. "You're asking me to believe in *magic?*" His braces glinted in the streetlights.

I nodded. Eddie flushed pink. Jaspar nuzzled sleepily against my shoulder. "What's magic, Matt?" he asked. Then he closed his eyes and fell asleep sitting up. Eddie sat still for about a minute, staring at Jaspar. Then he looked up.

"What does the other one do?" he asked suddenly, jerking his thumb down the street in the direction that Mr. Norris had run. "The bulldog, I mean. Does he dance or something? Sing songs? Tell fortunes?" He was grinning, sort of, and I knew he was trying to make a joke, trying to act like he was feeling normal again. I felt sorry for him, but I had to tell him.

"That's not really a bulldog," I said as calmly as I could. "It's Mr. Norris. I accidentally turned him into a dog."

Eddie turned almost sheet white. "Matt," he whispered. "Please tell me that was a joke."

"It's not a joke," I said. "I wish it were. I have to figure out how to change him back." I sounded pretty calm. I had to. If I got as upset as Eddie was, we would both just fall apart. Eddie was staring at me. I told him how it had happened. His glasses fogged up again. But he was starting to believe me, I could tell. "Mr. Norris can't talk. He just growls, but Jaspar can understand him," I finished. Eddie exhaled loudly.

"This is all too weird."

Just then Mrs. Hannover honked. It wasn't just one little beep this time, it was an urgent, come-here-quick, *beep, beep, beeeeeep* kind of honk. I jumped up, scooping Jaspar into my arms. I freed one hand and pulled Eddie into an awkward run toward the curb.

"I've spotted him, but I'm going to need help," Mrs. Hannover called as we got closer. "Climb in."

I pushed Eddie around the car and opened the door. He collapsed into the seat and Mrs. Hannover reached over and pulled him toward her so that I could get in. Jaspar sat on my lap. We were crammed in shoulder to shoulder. Mrs. Hannover's sports car was not very big.

Mrs. Hannover caught my eye and I nodded. She smiled. "So," she said, wheeling the car away from the curb, "Edward? Isn't it just wonderful about Jaspar?" Eddie's mouth opened and closed and opened and closed. He looked like a fish.

"Sure," he finally whispered. "Wonderful."

Mrs. Hannover patted his arm, without taking her eyes off the road. "You'll be fine, Edward. Just accept the idea that things you can't understand happen sometimes, and you'll be fine." Eddie nodded, and he wasn't quite as white anymore.

Mrs. Hannover drove a few blocks, then turned left. "Here," she said. "Mr. Norris was here just a few minutes ago. I would have tried to get him to come with me but he was . . . busy."

I leaned forward and looked out the window. Mrs. Hannover was slowing down in front of a Chinese restaurant. "I remembered this place was one of Mr. Norris's favorites," she said brightly. "Mr. Norris loves Chinese food."

"He does?" Eddie and I asked at the same time. I felt very strange for a second. I had never thought about Mr. Norris loving *anything*. Every time I saw him, he was either angry or grumpy or irritated or peeved or vexed or upset or just plain furious. I tried to picture him smiling. I couldn't.

Mrs. Hannover parked and turned off the engine. Jaspar pressed his nose against the window. I rolled it down and heard a dog growling. "There," I said, feeling relieved and worried at the same time. "There he is." Eddie leaned across to see.

Mr. Norris had cornered a man in a business suit

against the building. The man looked scared and he was talking in a low, desperate voice, trying to edge sideways along the building.

Mrs. Hannover slid out. "Mr. Norris is still busy," she said calmly. "Come on." I scrambled out awkwardly. Jaspar was heavy. I thought about leaving him in the car, but I was afraid to. So I stood up, holding him, ignoring my aching arms. Mrs. Hannover was already walking. Eddie followed us across the parking lot.

"Now, now, there you go, good doggie," the man was saying in a tense voice. "That's a good boy, just let me get by now and I'll . . . *ahg!*" He jumped back against the building as Mr. Norris snarled and moved closer. A small crowd of people had gathered. Jaspar wriggled in my arms and looked up at me.

"Mr. Norris says he's hungry and that he wants to go in and have dinner," he said softly.

I lowered my head like I was hugging him. "Don't say anything once we get closer to those people," I whispered. "Don't talk at all until I tell you it's all right. It's really important this time." He nodded somberly, looking like a little kid who doesn't understand what's going on. I hugged him again. Eddie was watching me. He reached out awkwardly and patted Jaspar's shoulder.

"You see the problem," Mrs. Hannover said quietly. I looked back at Mr. Norris, trying to think. He looked furious. He probably *was* hungry. Now that I thought about it, I sure was. Maybe he still thought this whole thing was a dream. Or maybe he was too scared and confused to think anything at all.

"Excuse me," Mrs. Hannover called out. "If everyone would stand back a little bit we can probably get him to calm down."

"Lady, I've been *trying* to stand back," the cornered man yelled back at her. "He won't let me move." He looked past us for a second, and smiled weakly. "It's about time," he said in a relieved voice. Then he looked back at Mrs. Hannover. "If he's yours, you can talk to the officer there." He pointed.

I looked back over my shoulder and groaned. A van with the words "Animal Control" painted on the side had pulled up to the curb and a man in a uniform had gotten out. He carried a long pole with a loop of thick rope dangling from one end. He was running toward us.

"Stay away from him," the man shouted as he got closer. He pushed his way past and before I could say anything, he had reached out and dropped the loop of rope over Mr. Norris's head. It tightened when the officer pulled back on the pole. Mr. Norris twisted and turned, trying to get the rope off. The man who had been cornered against the building ran inside the restaurant, then stood watching through the window.

"Take it easy, old boy," the officer said in a soothing voice, but he used the pole to keep Mr. Norris away from him, and away from anyone else.

"Stay back," he shouted to the people who stood watching. "He could have rabies."

People murmured, staring at Mr. Norris. Then the little crowd began to break up. I swallowed hard. If I didn't do something quick, Mr. Norris was going to end up in the back of that van.

"He doesn't have rabies," I said loudly. Mr Norris suddenly stood still, then he turned and looked at me. He made a soft whining sound and his tail drooped.

100

Instead of looking mean, he looked sad. Sad and lonely and scared.

The officer turned, holding the pole so that Mr. Norris couldn't move. "Is he your dog?"

I nodded. It wasn't exactly the truth, but it wasn't really a lie either. I did know that Mr. Norris didn't have rabies.

"I'll need to see proof that he's had his rabies vaccinations or I'll have to take him to the animal shelter," the officer said firmly. "Do you have his papers with you?"

"No," I answered, trying not to sound as worried as I was feeling. "But I'm sure he isn't sick or anything."

I glanced at Mrs. Hannover. She was watching me. Eddie was staring at Mr. Norris and he was looking pale again.

"If he hadn't bothered anyone I could let you take him, Miss," the officer said. He tugged at the pole gently, making Mr. Norris take a few steps, then a few more. "But since he was acting vicious, I have to take him in until you can prove he's been vaccinated." Mr. Norris growled and tried to get the rope off his neck. The officer pulled steadily, until Mr. Norris was moving toward the van again. "Rabies makes dogs act like this . . . mean and confused," the officer said over his shoulder. "If they bite someone, that person can get very sick."

He was walking a little faster, pulling Mr. Norris along. Mr. Norris growled again, but it was a whiny growl. A sad, frightened growl. And he was looking at me. I felt awful. Worse than awful. Mr. Norris in the animal shelter? As much as he hated dogs, he'd probably get in a fight. What if he got hurt? I couldn't prove he had had vaccinations. Would they think he should be put to sleep? My knees felt like Jell-O that had been left out on the counter all night. But what could I do? Grab the pole and run? I'd never get away.

At the curb, the officer was pulling Mr. Norris up a little ramp into the back of the van. He maneuvered around, until he was near the doors and Mr. Norris was way inside. He twisted his wrist and the rope was released. Then he jumped out holding the pole and turned back to slam a wire grating closed. He flipped the ramp up, secured it to the side of the van, then locked the wire grate shut with a key that hung from his belt. I hugged Jaspar, staring helplessly.

"I'll give you the address of the animal shelter and a copy of the report," the officer said, walking toward the front of the van. He pulled out a clipboard and started writing something.

I could hear Mr. Norris whining softly. He walked to the back of the van and looked out through the wire grating.

"Keep the officer busy for a minute," I told Eddie. He didn't move. I elbowed him. But he still didn't move. Mrs. Hannover took his arm.

"We have a few questions, officer," she sang out in a cheerful voice. The man turned to face her. I ducked back around behind the van.

Mr. Norris growled sadly. Jaspar wriggled in my arms and looked up at me. I glanced around. There were still a few people out in front of the restaurant, watching, but they were pretty far away. "Yes, Jaspar," I whispered. "Tell me what Mr. Norris said. But whisper. Like I am. Talk really quietly."

"He says it isn't a dream, is it?" Jaspar whispered in my ear. I walked closer to the wire grating.

"It isn't a dream, Mr. Norris," I said softly. "I don't know what to do, but I'll figure something out."

Mr. Norris growled.

"He says you better," Jaspar whispered. I shook my head, suddenly angry.

"You wouldn't be here if you had listened to us," I blurted out. "We tried to get you to go down to Mrs. Hannover's apartment."

Mr. Norris growled again, a long whimpery growl.

"He says to help him. Please."

That made my anger dissolve. It probably just about killed Mr. Norris to even be that nice—to say please. He was scared. Who wouldn't be? I leaned closer. "I promise we'll bring you home and I'll figure out how to change you back. I promise." My voice was scratchy, because I wasn't sure I could keep either one of those promises.

"Stand back, miss," the officer called around the side of the van. He started the engine and I watched Mr. Norris swaying with the motion of the van as it pulled away.

Eddie came to stand by me. "He said he has to finish his rounds, and he'll drop Mr. Norris off at the animal shelter around ten tonight. But we can't do anything until Monday morning. We can come pick Mr. Norris up Monday, if we bring his vaccination papers. If we don't have the papers, a vet will examine him on Tuesday, give him his shots, and Wednesday we can go get him."

"But today's Friday," I groaned. "Mr. Norris can't stay there until Wednesday. He'll never forgive me—he'll be so scared and so upset and . . . a veterinarian?" A sick, sinking feeling went through me.

"A vet might be able to tell that he's not a regular

103

dog," Eddie said, echoing my thoughts. I nodded, miserable.

"Look up, Mathilda," Mrs. Hannover said quietly. It took me a second to even understand what she had said. I glanced up. The moon was huge and silvery yellow through the trees.

"It's pretty," I said impatiently. Then I gulped and looked up again, suddenly understanding what she was talking about.

Eddie looked up at the moon, then back at me. "What's wrong?"

"The full moon," I squeaked. "If I don't change Mr. Norris back tonight, I'll have to wait until the next full moon—next month." My thoughts jumped around like someone standing barefoot on hot pavement. In a month, people would notice that Mr. Norris was gone. Someone might even call the police. He could get hurt or lost—anything could happen in a whole month. He'd never forgive me. Even if I changed him back next month—he'd never let me keep Jaspar. He might even try to sue my parents or something. The whole world would find out about Jaspar from the newspaper stories.

"We have to break him out tonight," Mrs. Hannover said in a low voice. I nodded. We had to. She was looking at her watch.

"We have an hour until ten o'clock and we are going to need every minute of it. My place first, then straight to the animal shelter. We want to be there when the officer brings him in. Hurry." I shifted Jaspar to one arm and grabbed Eddie's hand. Mrs. Hannover was already running toward her car.

CHAPTER ELEVEN

Mrs. Hannover made us eat. She had leftover chicken and she steamed broccoli and made a fast salad. I argued that we shouldn't take the time, but the minute I smelled food, I realized how *hungry* I was. She cut some meat up for Jaspar and set his plate on the floor.

While we ate she got out a big book and thumbed through the pages. "According to my almanac, we'll have about two hours of moonlight left if we get back here by eleven," she said, looking up. I nodded. Two hours to figure out how to change Mr. Norris back, get the magic done, and hope it works the first time. I squeezed my eyes shut for a second. It had taken weeks to prepare for Jaspar. Now I would have two hours—or even less if we took a long time getting Mr. Norris out.

I opened my eyes and looked around at the ferns, thinking about the first time I had come to Mrs. Hannover's apartment—back when my fingers tingling was the weirdest thing that had ever happened to me. It seemed like a hundred years ago.

The ferns were the same except that there were a

few flowers peeking out here and there now—fragile ones with odd, delicate petals. I knew the plants had to be growing in pots but they were so thick and green that it really did feel like I was standing in a clearing in a jungle.

Mrs. Hannover was smiling at me, and I flexed my arms up and down, trying to work out the cramps from carrying Jaspar. Eddie finished eating and stretched out on the floor and closed his eyes.

Mrs. Hannover disappeared through the ferns. I followed her into her kitchen, carrying our plates. If the living room was a jungle, the kitchen was a desert. There were three huge cactus plants standing along one wall. The old, ivory colored refrigerator was almost hidden by a dry-leafed manzanita plant with a dark twisted trunk.

"All right, it's nine-thirty," Mrs. Hannover announced when we came back into the living room. "It will take about fifteen minutes to drive to the animal shelter. That gives us ten to fifteen minutes to get ready."

Eddie sat up. Mrs. Hannover reached into the ferns and I heard a drawer slide open. There was furniture buried back in the ferns? She brought out a piece of paper and a pen.

"I've been to the animal shelter a few times over the years. There's a fence," she said, drawing a large rectangle on the paper, "and here's the building." She drew a wide V inside the square, and then a small circle at the point of the V. "That's the office. It's a big place. We'll have to figure out how to get Mr. Norris out once we get there, but that's the general layout. Now. What else do we need to do?"

"If we're going to be sneaking around in the dark

we ought to dress in black clothes,'' I said, knowing Eddie would frown. I ignored him. Mrs. Hannover nodded enthusiastically.

"Good idea. Run up to your place and change. Eddie can borrow a T-shirt of mine. His slacks are dark enough.'' Eddie groaned. I got up and headed for the door.

"Take your overnight bag back up to your place,'' Mrs. Hannover whispered into my ear. "By the time we get back, we'll need to use your windows for the moonlight. They are bigger and they face west.'' I nodded without answering. I knew why she was whispering. She didn't want to upset Eddie any more than he already was by talking about magic. "Bring a flashlight,'' she said in a louder voice.

I was already moving. I ran up the stairs into the lobby. By the time I was rummaging through my mother's drawers for her black turtleneck, I was already thinking about what I would need when we got back. I took *The Mad Inventor's Handbook* out of my overnight bag and opened it to the last section. I spread my notes out by it, and set the glass bowl on my desk with the salt container beside it. I scribbled a quick list. When we got back, I was going to be so rushed I might not be able to think straight. I folded the paper and left it on my desk. All that took me about two minutes. I was practically flying.

My flashlight was in a little drawer by my bed. I shoved it in my pocket. What else? I tore the bathroom drawers apart until I found the nail clippers. I clipped two of my own fingernails and put them by the bowl. "Spittle" would be easy this time, and for "genuine hair," I wanted to use Mrs. Hannover's, because it was gray like Mr. Norris's. I didn't know if that would

107

make a difference—it hadn't with Jaspar—but this was going to be different. I stood still for a second, thinking.

There was no way to get a real skeleton or skin, but I shouldn't need them. I was turning Mr. Norris back into a human being, after all, not *making* him from scratch. I couldn't think of anything else, so I pounded back through the apartment, locked the door, and tore for the elevator.

"Watch this, Matt," Jaspar said happily, when I got back down to Mrs. Hannover's. "Mrs. Hannover showed me how to act like a dog." He sat up straight for a second and I could tell he was concentrating. He began panting. After a few seconds, he raised a back paw to scratch at his ear. Then he wagged his tail a few times, and panted some more, and scratched his other ear. He barked once, softly. Then he sat up straight again. "See?"

I hugged him, looking gratefully at Mrs. Hannover. She winked. "And when do you act like a dog?" she asked Jaspar.

"Whenever there is anyone around me but my friends," Jaspar said confidently. "And I *only* talk to my friends," he added, like a kid showing off. I grinned and hugged him. His fur was warm. I felt better than I had for a long time. Eddie even smiled. He and Mrs. Hannover were both dressed in black. Mrs. Hannover's T-shirt fit him pretty well. He had rolled up the long sleeves. I wished desperately that we could just all spend the night teaching Jaspar new things, laughing, having fun. But of course we couldn't.

I cleared my throat. "Let's get going." Mrs. Han-

108

nover nodded. We went up the stairs and piled back into her little sports car. I glanced up at the moon as Mrs. Hannover pulled away from the curb. It was crossing the sky, getting lower. I realized suddenly that my hands hadn't tingled when I had opened *The Mad Inventor's Handbook.* They hadn't tingled the whole time I was getting things ready to change Mr. Norris back. Why? Maybe it was because I wasn't sure how I was going to change him back. Maybe it was because I wasn't sure I *could.* I tried not to worry about it.

Mrs. Hannover drove across town taking one shortcut after another, wheeling her little sports car around corners and down narrow alleys I had never noticed before. She kept glancing at her watch and looking at the stores we passed. Abruptly, she turned into the parking lot of a drugstore and got out without turning off the engine. Two minutes later she was back, carrying a small paper bag.

I wondered what was in the bag, but I was too preoccupied to ask. I was going over and over the magic chants in my mind, trying to figure out how I was going to change them. Eddie didn't say anything either. In fact, he was looking pretty pale again. Jaspar had fallen asleep on my lap. He didn't wake up when Mrs. Hannover put the car in gear and squealed out of the parking lot.

We drove around the animal shelter once, so we could get a look at it. It took up an entire block. It looked just like she had drawn it—except that when she had said there was a fence, I hadn't pictured a fence like this. It was six feet high, at least. It was chain link, topped with three strands of barbed wire. There was only one gate in it, a wide double gate at the entrance of the parking lot. It was closed and pad-locked.

On one side of the V-shaped building, there were pens full of dogs. You could hear them barking. There was a light on in the office, but the rest of the building was dark.

Mrs. Hannover looked at her watch. "Five of ten. Let's find a place to park."

She drove back around to the front of the building, then turned up the side street that followed the fence line.

"There," I said, pointing. There was a huge old tree that cast deep shadows on the street. Mrs. Hannover turned off the headlights and cut the engine. We coasted silently to a stop underneath the tree.

"Perfect," she murmured. "We can see the entrance, but no one will notice us." I nodded. Eddie sat stiffly between us. He hadn't said anything in so long that I was starting to worry about him.

Mrs. Hannover opened the paper bag and reached across Eddie to hand me something that looked like a tube of toothpaste. "Do your face and hands, then give it to Eddie," she whispered.

I got out. Jaspar woke up and I set him down on the ground. He yawned. "Don't make any noise and stay right here by me," I told him quietly, squinting to read the lettering on the tube. Halloween Black—remove with soap and water, it said.

I squeezed the tube and creamy black makeup oozed out. Bending over to use the rearview mirror, I smeared it on my face and neck, careful to do my eyelids and up high on my forehead. It would have been easier if my hand hadn't been shaking. The fine gravel on the side of the street crunched under my sneakers as I worked. Jaspar pressed against my leg. I did the backs of my hands, too. Then I handed the tube to Eddie and he knelt in front of the car mirror without saying anything. I could hear his breathing, though. I just hoped that he would be calm enough to help. I hoped *I* would be calm enough.

I leaned against the fence and whispered to Jaspar, explaining to him that we wanted to bring Mr. Norris home and that we had to wait until the van got there. I could hear Mrs. Hannover on the other side of the tree trunk, talking softly to Eddie. Even though the moon was still bright, the night seemed too dark and too quiet. What if the van had already come? I could see the night watchman standing in the lighted office. The rest of the building was dark. I counted windows along the side closest to us. There were twenty. It was a big building. But all the dogs were outside, I was pretty sure. They kept barking and barking.

"Here we go," Mrs. Hannover said, just loudly enough for me to hear her. Headlights swept up the block and turned toward the animal shelter. It was the van.

The officer got out and opened the gate, then drove through and parked in front of the lighted office. He used the pole and rope to take Mr. Norris out of the van. Mr. Norris wasn't growling or even trying to get the rope off his neck anymore. He walked along behind the officer without struggling at all. I watched very carefully, to see which pen they were going to put him in. But the officer led him into the lighted office area, instead. I heard the night watchman's voice just as the door closed behind them, but I couldn't understand what he said.

Mrs. Hannover came to stand just behind me. I

111

glanced back at her and she patted my arm. "They'll isolate him because they think he might be sick," she whispered. "Inside the building."

I shifted Jaspar onto my hip and freed one hand. I laced my fingers into the chain link fence and squeezed until it hurt. This was going to make it a lot harder. How would we get Mr. Norris out of the building? Lights came on in two of the windows. I counted. Nine windows from the office, on the side of the building we were on. But what was going on in there? I stretched up on my toes. Was that the room they were putting Mr. Norris in? For all I knew, those lights were from a room full of supplies and they had just stopped to get Mr. Norris a water dish or something before they turned around and walked all the way to the other side of the building.

I glanced up at the top of the fence, shifting Jaspar's weight onto my other hip. It was a huge building. We could wander around in there for an hour before we found Mr. Norris. I wasn't sure how we were going to get into the building, or how we were going to get Mr. Norris out, but I was sure of this much—unless we knew which room he was in, it was going to be almost impossible to rescue him before the watchman caught us.

Mrs. Hannover tapped me on the shoulder. She was holding out her arms. I handed Jaspar to her without saying anything. She was reading my mind again, and I was glad. I knew what had to be done.

"Don't," Eddie whispered as I started climbing. I ignored him, and I ignored my stiff, aching arms and I ignored my shivery nervousness. The strands of barbed wire on top of the fence snagged my shirt, but

112

I managed to get free. I climbed down about halfway then dropped to the other side, crouching low.

"This is too weird, Matt," Eddie hissed through the fence. "You'll get caught."

I faced him for an instant. "You have a better idea?" I hissed right back at him. He shook his head, looking miserable.

"I'll be right back," I told Jaspar in a gentler whisper. He nodded, blinking.

I ran, bending over so that I would be harder to see. I went straight across the parking lot, then across the strip of lawn in front of the building. All of a sudden I was there, pressed against the wall, peeking into one of the lighted windows.

The watchman and the officer were standing with their backs to the window, talking. Mr. Norris was huddled in a cage with clean sawdust spread on the bottom and a padlock on the door. I felt my stomach sinking. The watchman had a key tied to the end of a braided red cord. He was swinging it back and forth, smiling at something the officer had said. They moved toward the hallway and I saw the watchman reach toward the wall. The room went black. I was staring at nothing.

The key, I thought, panicking. Where would the watchman put that key? In his pocket? We had to get it. I started running.

I sprinted along the wall of the building, jumping little flower beds and trying not to make any noise. I skidded to a stop a foot or so away from the office windows. They were big, almost from the ground to the ceiling, and light poured out of them in huge rectangles that slanted across the lawn.

I could hear the two men talking as I inched my way

closer to the window. I leaned forward until I could see, every muscle in my body tense—ready to jerk back if they were looking toward me. But they weren't. Or at least the officer wasn't. I couldn't see the watchman.

I ran out into the parking lot, skirting the patches of light from the windows, and came up on the other side of the doors. From there, I could see the watchman, sitting on the edge of his desk. He still had the key in his hand. He was talking, twirling the key in circles. The officer said something that made him laugh. He walked behind his desk and hung the key up on a rack mounted on the wall. There were five or six keys there, but only that one had a red cord.

I exhaled in relief, and backed up, leaning against the building for a second. The key was where we could get it—if we could think of some way to get the watchman to leave his office. But how?

"See you tomorrow night," the officer said, and his voice was suddenly so loud, so close to me that my whole body went rigid. He had opened the door a crack, and had turned back to say good-bye to the watchman. I flattened myself against the wall and watched helplessly as the door swung open. I held myself still while the officer came out and walked toward the van. If he looked back, he would probably see me. But he didn't look back. I was almost starting to breathe again when I realized that the second he turned on his headlights, I'd look like an actor on a stage— standing right in front of the spotlights.

I ducked away from the building and ran through the dark toward the pens full of dogs. They barked at me, but they had been barking off and on the whole time, so I didn't think it would make anyone suspi-

114

cious. I crouched down and watched the officer get into the van. He hadn't seen me, I was pretty sure, but I didn't breathe again until he started the van and backed up. He stopped just outside the gates and closed them. I heard the lock click shut.

I stood up slowly. The dogs were still barking, but the watchman hadn't come out to check. They probably barked off and on, all night long—more at each other than anything else. I walked slowly along the pens. They all had strong latches, but none of them was locked. I stood still for a second. I was beginning to get the glimmer of an idea. I ran back toward the shadows where Jaspar and Mrs. Hannover and Eddie were waiting.

CHAPTER TWELVE

As soon as I was back over the fence, Jaspar jumped out of Mrs. Hannover's arms and leaped around like an excited puppy. I picked him up and motioned to the deepest shadows under the tree. We sat down and I started explaining.

"So we have to get the watchman out of the office," I finished up, whispering. "Maybe if we let the dogs in the pens out, the watchman would have to come outside. While he's chasing dogs around, I can sneak in and get Mr. Norris out."

Eddie looked at me over his glasses. They were spotted with the black makeup. "Weird plan, Matt."

"Edward . . ." Mrs. Hannover said quietly.

Eddie shrugged. "Well . . . I mean, it'd take the watchman at least a whole minute to figure out that he couldn't catch all those dogs by himself and then he'd come back into the office to telephone for help. He'd see Matt and call the police to come and arrest us. It's too simple. Don't you ever watch any spy movies?" he demanded, glaring at me.

"Sure, Eddie," I exploded, whispered fiercely. "We need listening devices and a helicopter and an under-

116

cover agent to infiltrate the animal shelter . . .'' I stopped suddenly, realizing what I had just said.

"That might work, you know," Mrs. Hannover said quietly.

I rubbed my face with my hands, thinking out loud. "If *one* dog wandered up to the office, the watchman would just think he was one of the dogs from the outside pens. If that dog ran from him, he just might chase it around long enough for us to get Mr. Norris out."

Eddie nodded and Mrs. Hannover was looking at me, smiling. But then I shook my head, worried. "Jaspar could get mixed up and scared. He's just too *young.*"

"No, I'm not," Jaspar said, sitting up so straight that he looked taller. I looked at him, imagining everything that might go wrong. My thoughts ran in circles, arguing with themselves. I hated the idea of putting Jaspar in danger, but we had do something to rescue Mr. Norris. I looked up at the moon. It was a lot lower in the sky now.

"Eddie will be with him, or close by, the whole time," Mrs. Hannover said calmly.

"Me?" Eddie bleated. Mrs. Hannover and I both jumped. "Me?" he repeated, whispering this time.

Mrs. Hannover nodded. "I'll be the lookout and the getaway driver," she told us, her eyes twinkling.

I looked at Eddie. "You have to help. Jaspar will distract the watchman and lead him away from the office and the telephone. I'll go in and get Mr. Norris out. You'll be the troubleshooter. Make sure that Jaspar doesn't get caught. You can just hide along the building somewhere and be ready in case he needs you." Eddie was shaking his head.

I leaned forward, making him look at me. "Eddie, we need you. I couldn't stand it if anything happened to Jaspar."

Eddie looked down. "Me either," he said, so quietly that I wasn't sure I had heard him right. Then he looked at me again. "Okay. I'll do it. Even if you are the world's biggest weirdette."

I hugged him so quickly that he didn't have time to push me away until it was over. He smiled, sort of, and pushed his glasses up. They were smeared with black now.

We ran through the plan twice, to make sure that Jaspar understood it. He looked very serious, nodding and listening. "All right," Mrs. Hannover said after the final run-through. "Jaspar, tell Mathilda what the plan is."

Jaspar looked up at me. "Eddie and you and me will go in," he said softly. "We will be really, reeeally quiet. Then you and Eddie are going to hide. I am going to go up to the windows and bark like this . . ." He made a few whispery barking sounds. "But I'll do it much louder. When the watchman comes out, I run around and around farther and farther from the doors. He won't catch me, Matt." Jaspar jumped in a little circle, looking exactly like a frisky dog, and I knew he was trying to reassure me. "Then, when you call me, I come to you and we all go home," he finished looking so proud of himself that I smiled.

"That's right," I whispered, leaning down to hug him. When I stood up, there was a streak of black along Jaspar's side. Mrs. Hannover took the tube out of her pocket touched up my face. I was so nervous I could barely stand still. But I was determined, too. We would get Mr. Norris out. We had to. I glanced at the moon. "Let's go."

The fence seemed even higher than it had before. I stared at it, feeling my determination fade a little. How could we get Jaspar over it? Whoever was carrying him would have to climb one-handed.

"I can get through down here," Jaspar said softly. And he began digging. I watched him, astonished.

"He probably has most of the instincts of a dog," Mrs. Hannover whispered to me. I nodded. It made sense, but watching Jaspar digging made me feel strange. It was like seeing him nod, or hearing him talk—but the other way around this time.

The ground was soft and in about fifteen seconds, Jaspar was wriggling under the fence. I climbed the wire and dropped down on the other side. Eddie was right behind me.

He pushed his glasses up. "This is weird, Matt." His eyes looked huge against his blackened skin. I forced myself to think.

"Take Jaspar to the middle of the parking lot where it's dark," I whispered into his ear. "Count to fifty before you do anything. I need time to get close to the office." I knelt and reminded Jaspar to be careful. He nodded and nuzzled into my shoulder. I stood up and shivered, then I ran into the darkness.

I got as close to the office windows as I dared—this time I wouldn't take the chance of being seen when the watchman came out. I couldn't stop shivering.

Suddenly, Jaspar ran into the lawn, straight into the big rectangles of light that shone from the office windows. He ran right up to the door, barking. His bark sounded a little funny at first, but it got louder each time he barked. I crossed my fingers, my stomach churning. If anything happened to him I would never forgive myself.

Jaspar ran in circles, then he ran back and forth. He ran out into the parking lot, then back to the door. Finally, he stood right in front of the office door, barking. I heard a scraping sound, like a chair being pushed back, and then the door opened. Jaspar dashes away.

"Hey," the watchman called out from the doorway. "Come here, fella. Come on. Where did you come from?"

Jaspar circled at a dead run, flashing through the rectangles of light from the windows, past the watchman, and back into the darkness again. I held my breath.

"Come on," the watchman called. "Come on, come here now." He clapped his hands.

Jaspar made a smooth, wide turn in the parking lot then flashed back into the light, running toward him. I clenched my teeth. If Jaspar got too close . . .

But then he angled off to one side and ran away again. The watchman stepped outside, chuckling. "Full of pep, aren't you? Well, it's not raining or anything. You ought to be all right out there until morning." He chuckled again and went back inside.

As the door closed, I hit the side of the building in frustration. He had to come out. He just had to. Jaspar tore in circles, barking constantly, coming closer and closer to the door each time. His bark was beginning to sound hoarse, but he kept it up, getting louder and louder.

The watchman didn't come out.

Jaspar went around and around, barking so loudly that it hurt my ears. He came to a stop in front of the door and barked, tense and ready to dash away.

120

But the watchman didn't come out.

Jaspar flung himself against the door, barking.

The watchman didn't come out.

Jaspar backed away from the door and took a run at it, jumping as high as he could, clawing at the wood and barking frantically. I could see his sides heaving. He was getting tired and his barking sounded raspy, as if it hurt him to keep it up. But he did. He jumped against the door twice more, barking madly, breathing so hard I could hear him gasping between barks. The watchman still didn't come out.

"Come ouuut," Jaspar screamed suddenly in a hoarse voice. "You have to come out so we can save Mr. Norris!"

I almost jumped out of my skin. Jaspar sat down abruptly, looking confused and guilty, one paw up against his mouth. He looked exactly like a kid talking in class who just realized that the teacher is standing right behind him. I swallowed hard, too scared to move. The door was opening.

"Is there somebody out here?" the watchman called cautiously, glancing down at Jaspar, then looking back out toward the dark parking lot. He flipped on a big flashlight and I mashed myself flat against the wall as he swept the powerful beam around. I heard a faint scraping of sand out in the parking lot and I knew Eddie was running to get out of the way. Jaspar was still sitting in front of the door, looking confused and scared. The watchman reached for him. I almost yelled then, but before I could, Jaspar scrambled backward, remembering what he was supposed to do.

Jaspar ran a few steps, then stopped, looking back, waiting for the watchman to chase him. The watchman kept shining his big flashlight around slowly, searching through the shadows, looking for the person who had yelled at him through the closed door. Jaspar had caught his breath and he darted back toward the watch-man, bumping into his leg before he turned and ran away again, barking hoarsely.

"Hey, shut up," the watchman yelled. He wasn't chuckling anymore. "All that barking is getting on my nerves. You've got me thinking that I'm hearing voices."

Jaspar ran through the patches of light on the lawn, coming close to the watchman, sprinting so fast that his legs blurred. The watchman made a grab for him and missed. Jaspar slid to a stop and sat down, fifteen feet away from him. "Come *on,*" the watchman said sternly, walking across the lawn. Jaspar jumped up and ran another ten feet and sat down again, still barking. He looked back over his shoulder as the watchman followed.

"I've had enough of this," the watchman said. He grabbed for Jaspar again, but Jaspar sprang into a run—then sat down twenty feet farther away, panting and waiting. The watchman walked toward him, talking in a low, cajoling voice.

I forced my feet to move. Fast. For every step the watchman took away from the office door, I took three or four toward it. When I reached the door I glanced back. The watchman was still following Jaspar, talking and calling, and shining his flashlight around. His back was toward me. *Now,* I told myself, and ran through the door.

I skidded like a hockey player on the slick linoleum. For a second, I probably looked like a cartoon char-acter, running without getting anywhere. Then I was around the corner and sliding to a stop by the watchman's desk. The key was still there, hanging by the red cord. I snatched it off the hook and took off down the hall, counting the doors I passed. They were all standing open. The hallway was longer than I had expected, but I finally came to the ninth door and slid into the darkened room.

I pulled my flashlight out of my pocket, and almost dropped the key. I turned the flashlight on and kept the beam low, on the floor. "Mr. Norris?" I whispered, but I was breathing so hard it came out more like "Mishternorse?". I heard a growl, and swung the flashlight across three empty cages. Then I saw him.

He was standing up, his wrinkly gray face pressed against the front of his cage. I fumbled with the key. "Mr. Norris, we have to hurry." He snarled at me.

"I don't know what you're saying," I told him as I fit the key into the lock. "But what we have to do now is sneak out of the building without the watchman seeing us. Eddie and Jaspar are distracting him. Mrs. Hannover is waiting for us." I turned the key, but I was afraid to open the door. Mr. Norris was pressed so hard against the wire that I was scared. Would he just run away again? That was the absolute *last* thing we needed. I could hear Jaspar's shrill barking outside. How much longer would the watchman chase him around? Or had he already given up and was on his way back?

Mr. Norris growled and shoved against the wire. "I won't let you out unless you promise not to run away," I said frantically. "You have to stay with me. Understand? Nod if you promise."

Mr. Norris snarled again, showing his teeth, but he backed away from the wire door and nodded. It looked even stranger than when Jaspar did it, because Mr.

123

Norris's neck was short and thick. When he nodded his whole body moved.

I swung the cage door open and he scrambled out, his eyes wide and wild-looking. I imagined myself in his situation for a second. I'd be terrified, too.

"It's going to be all right," I said, patting him gently on the shoulder. "Just calm down and we'll be home soon." He turned and stared at my hand. I pulled my hand away, blushing.

There was an explosion of barking outside. It wasn't just Jaspar—it was the dogs in the pens, too. I moved toward the door with Mr. Norris right behind me, growling low in his throat. Over all the barking outside, I heard one quick, short yelp from Jaspar.

I started to run. Mr. Norris took a little longer to get going on the slick floor, but once he did, he caught up. We made it down the long hall and slid into the office almost side by side. I hung the key back up and whirled around. The windows looked black from inside. Whatever we were going to run into, we would probably be better off running into it at high speed. I sprinted toward the door and hit it like a runaway train. Mr. Norris was right behind me. We pounded across the sidewalk and onto the lawn.

"Get away," I heard the watchman shouting in the darkness near the dog pens. "Let go now. What's wrong with you?" I slowed to a trot. I could see his flashlight beam, swinging downward.

I heard Jaspar yelp again, high and panicky. I veered to the right and stumbled into Mr. Norris. He growled, but I ignored him. What was wrong with Jaspar?

"Get away from me," the watchman shouted again. His flashlight beam was turning in crazy arcs, slicing

124

the night. I heard the strange hoarse bark again and I sprinted, ready to do whatever I had to to help Jaspar.

One second I was running hard. The next I was spinning around. "Matt," Eddie said urgently as he held on to my arm, dragging me to a stop. "Jaspar's in trouble. Look."

I tried to shake my arm free. "I know, that's where I—"

"Look," Eddie insisted. His fingers were digging into my wrist. Jaspar barked again. My eyes were beginning to adjust to the darkness and I could see the watchman over by the pens of dogs, trying to walk back toward the office. He couldn't, because Jaspar had grabbed the cuff of his trousers and was hanging on.

"You'd have never gotten Mr. Norris out, if Jaspar hadn't done that," Eddie panted. "The watchman would have gone back in a long time ago. He's been hitting at him, too, with that flashlight. But if you just go tearing up there, he'll grab you. Where's Mr. Norris?" Eddie demanded suddenly, looking around. A growling sound came out of the darkness close to us. "Oh," Eddie said.

I stared as the watchman tried to pull his pants leg free from Jaspar's stubborn grip. "You two go back, go wait with Mrs. Hannover," I told Eddie. Mr. Norris growled again. "Go *on,*" I said, pushing him, and then I was running again, crossing the dark parking lot at an angle that would keep me from the watchman's flashlight beam.

Eddie was right. If the watchman grabbed me, I'd be in big trouble, but even worse than that, we'd never get Mr. Norris changed back in time. If I just yelled at Jaspar to let go, the watchman would hear me and chase us. With that powerful flashlight he could watch us go over the fence and call the police with a description of Mrs. Hannover's car. We probably wouldn't make it ten blocks before they caught us. So far, all the watchman knew was that a dog had gotten out of the pens and was acting goofy. We had to keep it that way.

What we needed now was *another* distraction, one that would cause so much confusion that Jaspar could let go and we could run for it without being seen.

The dogs in the pens were excited by all the commotion, barking and jumping against the gates. The first latch was stiff, but I finally got it open. Ten or fifteen dogs poured out, brushing my legs as they streamed around me. The second latch was easier. The third one practically fell open. I flung the gates wide and ran back toward Jaspar.

I skidded to a stop in the parking lot, watching. The dogs from the pens were circling the watchman now, growling and barking and running. I started forward, trying to think of a way to attract Jaspar's attention. It was time for him to let go. We had to run. Suddenly Jaspar released his grip and jumped backward, barking loudly at the dogs. They all stopped running, instantly, like they were playing freeze tag. Then a big collie sprang forward and pushed the watchman over, slowly, almost gently. He fell onto the grass, shouting at the dogs to get away. A Saint Bernard lumbered over and lay across his legs. The collie lay down on his chest and two other big dogs lay down on his outspread arms. The flashlight rolled down the slope, its beam pointing eerily toward me. The watchman struggled helplessly, making strange sounds.

For an instant, I was terrified that the dogs were

126

attacking him, but as I ran closer, scooping Jaspar up in my arms, I saw the collie licking his face. The watchman's eyes were scrunched closed and he was turning his head back and forth. A dachshund was yipping at the Saint Bernard, dashing back and forth. The collie looked up and barked at me.

"He says get going," Jaspar said in my ear. "Don't worry. They won't hurt him, Matt."

I swayed on my feet. The dachshund was staring at me too, still yipping loudly. "He says thanks for the fun," Jaspar said softly. He nuzzled into my shoulder. "I was scared. It's a good thing they helped when I asked them to. Did we save Mr. Norris, Matt?"

I shook my head to clear my thoughts. Well, of course Jaspar could talk to the dogs. It was more understandable than his being able to talk to me, wasn't it?

The collie looked straight into my eyes and barked once more. "He says get going, stupid," Jaspar translated.

That snapped me out of it. I started running toward the fence, toward the old tree, toward my friends. I could hear Mrs. Hannover's little sports car's engine running, and I quit thinking about anything except getting home.

CHAPTER THIRTEEN

We staggered and stumbled into my apartment. "We look weird," Eddie said when I flipped on the lights. I nodded. You can't argue with the truth.

Jaspar's coat was streaked with black from my face and hands. Eddie looked exhausted. His glasses were smeared and sliding down his nose. Mrs. Hannover was smiling cheerfully, her eyes twinkling like a little kid's at a circus. Mr. Norris was growling almost constantly—but Jaspar had stopped translating everything he said. Mr. Norris had growled all the way home. He was furious with me. All he wanted to do was get changed back so he could yell at me in English.

I set Jaspar down gently before I went down the hall to wash my face and hands. When I was done, Eddie cleaned up, and Mrs. Hannover used a washcloth to get the black makeup off Jaspar's fur. All I wanted to do in the whole world was hug Jaspar and then sleep for about two days. But I couldn't. I had to get busy.

First, I had to make sure that everyone was far enough away so that the magic didn't do anything it wasn't supposed to this time. I would have to work in the living room, because that's where the biggest windows were that faced west—toward the moon hanging low in the sky.

"I'll put Jaspar and Eddie to bed," Mrs. Hannover said, "then I'll just read in your room and stay out of the way." I nodded, glad that she seemed to know what I was thinking.

Mr. Norris was pacing back and forth across the living room, glancing at me and growling quietly. I hugged Jaspar good night and told him how brave and good and amazing he was. I didn't want to let go of him. He yawned.

"We did it, Matt," he said in a sleepy voice. "We rescued Mr. Norris."

I nodded, afraid to say what I was thinking. What if I couldn't change him back? Mr. Norris had never been nice to me, but he didn't deserve to be a bulldog the rest of his life. But if I did change him back, he would probably make us move. We probably wouldn't be able to find an apartment that would allow Jaspar. What if Mr. Norris told people about Jaspar? What if I changed him back and he just went upstairs and called the police?

Mrs. Hannover took Eddie and Jaspar down the hall. I followed them into my room and got out a sleeping bag that Eddie could use. Feeling confused and miserable, I gathered up *The Mad Inventor's Handbook,* the glass bowl, and everything else I would need. Eddie stretched out on the floor and Jaspar curled up next to him. Mrs. Hannover switched on my reading light and lay down on my bed. Her eyes sparkled when I asked her for three strands of her hair. As I tiptoed out, Eddie and Jaspar were already sound asleep.

I went into the living room and found the right page in *The Mad Inventor's Handbook.* While I got things ready, I explained to Mr. Norris why we had to hurry. He looked out the window at the moon, then growled and came to sit near me. The moon was low. I spread out my notes, going over the chants, forcing myself to concentrate.

I looked at the list I had scribbled before we left for the animal shelter. "Mrs. Hannover's hair, skip dog description, describe Mr. Norris, rewrite final chant," I had written. I picked up my pen and a fresh sheet of paper. Using the magic chants in *The Mad Inventor's Handbook* as a guide, I wrote a chant that I thought would work. Instead of using a description of a dog, as I had for Jaspar—or a description of a monster, as *The Mad Inventor's Handbook* did—I wrote a chant about a grumpy-looking gray-haired man.

I was pretty sure that I could change him back if I just repeated the potion and all the hand motions and left out all the chants except the first three and the one I had just written. And I would have to include the part in which I said I believed in the magic and wanted it to work with all my heart.

I looked at my notes. The potion would be slightly different. I set out the clippings from my fingernails and everything else I would need. I could feel my heart thudding as I worked. I was scared. My hands still weren't tingling and Mrs. Hannover hadn't sneezed once. I glanced out the window. The moon was so low I didn't have time to worry, I had to get going.

I told Mr. Norris that I had made Jaspar with magic and that if I was going to change him back, he had to cooperate with me. "I know this all seems strange to you, Mr. Norris," I said carefully, "but you have to do exactly what I tell you to do. Just stay very still while I say the chants, and when I put a little of the potion on your face, hold still. All right?"

He nodded, growing a little. I took a deep breath and began the potion, starting with "one portion of clear water," then the salt. I read the words from *The Mad Inventor's Handbook* then added the "second portion" of water. I made the motions with my hands that I was supposed to make. Mr. Norris growled softly as he watched me. I moved closer to the windows, where the moonlight came in, and I let the light fall on the bowl. I added my two fingernail clippings to the potion. When I put in a little of my own "spittle," Mr. Norris made an odd growling sound, but I ignored him. That's what worked, and I wasn't about to try to do it any other way now.

One long strand of Mrs. Hannover's hair went in the bowl next. After each thing I made the magic hand motions and said the words the book told me to say. Then I asked Mr. Norris to sit in the moonlight on the floor and he did, growling. I set the bowl just in front of him and walked around him three times, repeating the magic words, just like the instructions said to do.

I sat down in front of Mr. Norris, facing the window, in a patch of moonlight, just like I had with Jaspar. I held two long gray hairs of Mrs. Hannover's between the third and fourth fingers of my right hand. Then I picked up the bowl in both hands and dribbled a little of the potion on Mr. Norris's face. When I finished, I held the bowl in my lap and I tried very, very hard to believe that it would work—that it *was* working. "I believe in magic," I whispered. I did. After all, I had seen proof that it worked. "I believe in magic and I want this to work with all my heart, my mind, and my will."

131

Concentrating as hard as I could, I read the chant I had written very slowly, careful to pronounce every single word exactly right. As I said the final words, the water in the bowl was supposed to start to bubble and steam—but it didn't. I raised the bowl over my head anyway—but nothing happened.

Nothing at all.

Mr. Norris growled, glaring at me.

I knew it wasn't working. I lowered the bowl. My eyes were burning and my throat ached. There wasn't much time left. I started rereading my notes, trying to figure out what had gone wrong. Mr. Norris growled.

"I don't know why it didn't work," I told him. My voice was squeaky and my hands were shaking. I pulled *The Mad Inventor's Handbook* towards me. What if I couldn't make it work? What if Mr. Norris was a bulldog forever? It was probably horrible not being able to talk. He hated dogs. He absolutely hated *being* one, I was sure. Unless I could change him back, his whole life would seem like a nightmare. I ran my shaking fingers back and forth across the page, trying to concentrate. I couldn't see anything that I had done wrong. I had followed the directions pretty exactly. I felt pure, cold panic rising in my throat. No. Not just panic. It was a tangle of feelings that added up to panic. I closed my eyes. Mr. Norris growled, and he sounded angry.

"I'm doing the best I can," I managed to say around the lump in my throat. I opened my eyes but I couldn't stand to look at him, growling like that. I jumped up and ran down the hall. Mrs. Hannover would know what was wrong. She would help me.

My reading light was still on. Mrs. Hannover was lying on my bed, with her eyes closed and one of my

132

books laid carefully beside her. She was asleep. I stared at her calm, Gypsy grandmother's face and I knew there was no reason to wake her up. It wasn't her responsibility to straighten things out. It was mine. Besides, Mrs. Hannover couldn't help me. I knew what was wrong. Somewhere in the tangle of feelings that had made me feel panicky was a huge feeling of relief. The magic hadn't worked because I didn't *want* it to work. It was that simple. And that complicated. I flipped off the light and tiptoed out.

Back in the living room, I faced Mr. Norris. "I know what's wrong," I whispered. Mr. Norris was glaring at me, his bulldog face scrunched into even more wrinkles than usual. He growled.

"I can't make the magic work unless I want it to, I mean *really* want it to work. Mr. Norris, unless you promise that you'll let me keep Jaspar, and that you'll never tell anyone that he isn't just a normal dog—I can't change you back." I looked straight into Mr. Norris's eyes. "I love Jaspar, and I can't let you hurt him. Jaspar thinks you're his friend," I added, without quite knowing why I said it. He growled, low and grumpy and for so long that I thought he would never stop. I knew what he was doing, he was giving me a lecture.

"I can't understand you," I said, shaking my head. "But it doesn't matter. Unless you promise, I can't make the magic work even if I think I *should.*" I swallowed. "And I'm glad," I blurted out suddenly. "I did everything I could to help you, and so did Eddie and so did Mrs. Hannover. So did Jaspar. Especially Jaspar. He's the one who kept the watchman from catching us. You think your rules are so important. Well, they aren't. Friends are a lot more important."

I was breathing hard. Mr. Norris had stopped growling. I glanced out the window. The moon was sitting right on the horizon.

Very, very slowly, staring at me, Mr. Norris nodded. Twice.

My eyes flooded with tears. "You promise? You won't make us move and you won't ever tell anyone about Jaspar?"

He nodded again. I leaned forward and hugged him hard. He wriggled away from me, growling a little. I tried to stop crying, but I couldn't. If I could keep Jaspar, and Mr. Norris would help keep him safe, then everything was perfect. Or it would be if I could just make the magic work.

I wiped my eyes and reached for my notes. My hand brushed *The Mad Inventor's Handbook* and started tingling all the way up to my wrist. I jumped up to get fresh water.

This time the chants seemed easier to say and the moonlight even seemed to get a little brighter. The water began to heat up like it had when Jaspar was coming to life. When I finished I stared at Mr. Norris, holding my breath. He started to shimmer. He got blurry and bigger, then shimmery and taller. Then he was standing there, looking just like himself.

He flexed his fingers wide, then crunched his hands into fists—then opened them again. He lifted one foot and stared at his shoe. He took a single step and stopped, touching his face, running his hands across his forehead, his nose, his chin, his chest.

"You look perfect," I breathed. "Do you feel all right?" I was so tired that I could hardly talk.

He swung his arms around a few times. "I think so. I seem to be . . . fine."

"Oh, Mr. Norris, I'm so glad," I whispered.

"Matt?" Jaspar's voice came down the hallway. He came into the living room and stopped abruptly, staring at Mr. Norris.

"It's all right," I reassured him. "This is Mr. Norris."

Jaspar walked up to Mr. Norris, a puzzled expression on his face. He sniffed at his pant leg, then his hand. Then he sat down and looked up. "You look different now," he said slowly. "But it's you."

Mr. Norris reached down and patted Jaspar's head, then pulled his hand back quickly, as if he was embarrassed. He looked absolutely perfectly normal. Grumpy, I mean. He was glaring at me. "No other rules are changed, do you understand?"

I nodded.

"You can keep Jaspar, but there's still no running in the halls, no playing in the elevator, nothing like that at all."

"I promise," I said, nodding so hard that I made myself feel a little dizzy. I couldn't stop nodding. I thought I might start crying again. I was so tired, and so relieved.

Then I saw Eddie. He was standing in the hall, looking in at us. "I watched him change," he breathed. "You woke me up when you came in. I was right. You're the weirdest person I ever knew." He pointed at *The Mad Inventor's Handbook*. "You learned how to do all that from that book?"

I nodded.

"Weird," he said. "I didn't believe you before. Not really. I was underestimating how weird you really are."

I stared at him. Everyone was back to normal, even Eddie.

"I'm so glad," I whispered.

"This is all very hard to believe," Mr. Norris was saying. His voice sounded like it was coming from someplace far away. I leaned closer to hear him better. He reached out to catch me. That's when I realized that I wasn't leaning, I was falling. I didn't care. I was so tired and it was all over and everything was wonderful. All I wanted in the whole world was to go to sleep.

CHAPTER FOURTEEN

My mother and father came back from New York together Sunday night. It was a surprise—my father had gotten a few extra days off before he had to go back to Mexico. My mom called me at Eddie's when they got to the airport, so we met them downstairs in the lobby.

When they opened the doors, Jaspar and I were sitting on the floor by the elevators. I jumped up and ran to hug them. I was still a little nervous about things. I knew Jaspar wouldn't talk around them. Mrs. Hannover and I had spent hours explaining to him why it would be dangerous for him to talk around anyone except his "special" friends. And Mr. Norris had kept his promises—even though he looked a little sick whenever he saw Jaspar and me in the hallways. But what if he was just waiting for my parents to get home?

My mother was hugging me when she noticed Jaspar.

"Matt, why is that . . . that . . . ?"

"Dog," I said, since she couldn't seem to find the right word.

"Dog," she echoed. She was smiling her stiff, nervous smile. "But Mr. Norris won't . . . I mean he'll . . ."

My dad held out his arms and I hugged him. Hard.

Just then the elevator doors opened and Mr. Norris got out. When he saw us he frowned. Jaspar ran up to him. He's always glad to see Mr. Norris. Mr. Norris usually pats his head a little, when he thinks no one's watching. Mr. Norris glanced at me and then said hello to my parents. I held my breath.

"Mathilda seems to have a . . ." my mother began.

"Dog," I said again, staring at Mr. Norris. My heart was thudding. Mr. Norris could just tell them all about it right now. He could break his promises and ruin everything.

Mr. Norris cleared his throat. "I've made a special exception to the rules for Mathilda," he said slowly. He kept glancing down at Jaspar. "Since she's home alone fairly often after school, I thought it might be a good idea if she had a . . . dog," he finished, barely whispering the last word. I wanted to run and hug him, but I caught myself.

"Oh, thank you, Mr. Norris," I blurted. My parents were staring at me. "For explaining, I mean," I added, trying to calm down. Mr. Norris shook my father's hand and then he walked toward the lobby doors.

"Jaspar likes Mr. Norris a lot," I said, loudly enough for him to hear me as he left. He hesitated for an instant before he pushed the doors open and went out.

"Jaspar?" my mother repeated. I nodded happily. My mother nodded, looking at Jaspar. "He looks almost exactly like the picture on that old book. Where did you get him, Matt?"

"I brought him home from the animal shelter," I told her without pausing. That was what Eddie and Mrs. Hannover and I had decided to tell people. My father grinned. I was so happy I could barely stand it. "Mom and Dad, meet Jaspar," I said proudly. Jaspar sat down and lifted his right paw for them to shake.

When my father straightened up he smiled. "You're lucky. Most dogs aren't as smart as Jaspar is."

I was grinning so widely that it hurt my face. "I know," I told him. "I know."

Since that morning, life has been great. Grady came over one day to meet Jaspar. When she shook hands with him she said, "He's as cute as a little button."

Jaspar stays with Mrs. Hannover when I'm at school. I can't wait until summer so I can be with him all day. He loves to go to the park, and he loves to talk to dogs there. I want to take him out to Grady's ranch someday so that he can tell me what Rico has to say. Rico must have wondered why in the world I was cutting his toenails that day.

After all the excitement died down, my mother remembered the pattern she had given me. I told her I had given it to a friend, who needed it more than I did now. She only smiled. She didn't even get too mad when I told her I had borrowed her black turtleneck and ripped it a little. In fact, my mother seems sure that having Jaspar is teaching me responsibility. Maybe it is, I don't know. I just know that I'm happy.

Even Eddie is nicer now. Not much nicer. I mean, he still says, "You're the weirdest person I've ever known," instead of good-bye when we get to school every morning. But he also says he wants to help me with the project I'm planning.

I used to think up projects when I was lonely and

bored. Now, it's just the opposite. I have Eddie and Mrs. Hannover and Grady and Shernoz—and Jaspar. Especially Jaspar. He jumps up and runs in circles when I get home from school, and we take long walks every afternoon. He's the best friend I've ever had in my life. Whenever I feel bad about something, I hug him and feel better.

So I'm not lonely anymore, and I can't imagine ever being bored with Jaspar around. But I'm working on the most incredible project I've ever thought of in my whole life. It'll work, too, I bet. My hands tingled this morning and Mrs. Hannover has been sneezing a lot. Mr. Norris won't like it, but magic can't be against the rules.